Jacks Hill Road

A Jamaican Novel

Jennifer Grahame

Jacks Hill Road
A Jamaican Novel

This book is a work of fiction. Names, characters, places and incidents either are products of the author's imagination or are used fictitiously. Any resemblance to actual events or persons, living or dead, is entirely coincidental.

www.jennifergrahame.com

Book Cover design by: Copy Cat
www.copycatjm.com

Portrait of Louise (Back Cover) Original painting
By Jennifer Grahame. Acrylic on canvas

DEDICATION

For Joyce

TABLE OF CONTENTS

CHAPTER 1

Lime Cay

Louise appeared around the bend and paused to gather her strength for the walk up the last hill. It was only seven in the morning and already the sun felt hot on her bare head. "Lawd, I hate Monday mornings," she muttered.

The dishes from Friday's dinner would be piled high in the sink, the laundry strewn with wet bathing suits and every bath tub in the house full of sand.

Buses rarely ran on time up Jacks Hill Road forcing Louise to walk most of the way. It was hard, the knees of her fat legs bawled in pain as she trudged heavily up the hill. Puffing by the time she got to her employer's house her foul mood grew darker by the minute. Louise stopped at the gate to catch her breath and surveyed the yard. The beauty of the landscape always surprised her, coming from the dirt and rock stone of the downtown area, the brightly coloured garden threatened a headache. She looked to the heavens and pleaded for the Lord's help to get her through another Monday.

"Miss Louise, morning Miss Louise," shouted Denton, the 'half crack' gardener, as he rushed toward her.

"Rass claat man you want to give me a heart attack this early morning? What you want?"

"Some needle and thread," said Denton, as he pulled a long green garden hose.

***

Behind him "a long thread and a very big needle to sew up every dog batty in here this morning. I is very tired of all the dog shit in the yard Miss Louise as I clean one shit I find a next one!"

"Listen to me man, come, out of my way and allow me to do my work in here this morning. When the dogs explode, you will have even more shit to clean, you idiot," declared Louise as she pushed past him to work the locks on the back door.

"Then Miss Louise, you think if we get rid of some of the dogs they will miss them? One or two dogs is all right but why dem have to have ten?"

"Listen Denton, I have no time for any fool, fool argument now," slamming the back door in his face. She leaned against the door and slowly surveyed the kitchen. The mess was more than usual, every glass, plate and pot was dirty and empty wine bottles lined the counter while Mrs. Carmen Pottinger's bikini bottoms circled slowly above, hung from a blade of the ceiling fan.

***

Upstairs, Dan Pottinger rolled over at the first clatter of plates, his head throbbed something awful. If Louise was in the kitchen that meant that it was after seven. He had a meeting this morning and could not afford to be late; he cautiously opened an eye and looked at the clock and sighed, 7:45, traffic will be bumper to bumper, it made no sense rushing. He was too drunk last night to remember to set the alarm clock and his damn fool of a wife was no better. He looked at her now; she was asleep on her back snoring softly, drool ran down her chin.

Like most Sundays, yesterday began with their weekly trip to the cays on the boat. As usual, their children Elizabeth, 16, and Bradley, 14, had disappeared as soon as the boat docked. The water was choppy and less clear than usual; but by the time Dan and Carmen had had their first drink, the sea became amazingly calm. A typical Sunday on Lime Cay, the boats were lined up and bobbed on their moorings, as friends laughed and chatted about the week's events, they swapped stories, drinks and food. It was a perfect Sunday until the arrival of big mouth Basil.

Basil Thomas was a big man with a bigger voice. He could not whisper and had no control over the boom of his voice. Dan saw Basil step from the canoe and thought about trying to hide.

"Dan!" He shouted, "Dan!" as he swam up to Dan's boat. "Permission to come aboard, Sir." Basil was the accountant at Dan's Insurance Company, and Dan had been trying for years to fire him.

"Come aboard man, you are welcome anytime," he said through gritted teeth. Dan had fantasies of drowning the man.

Basil nearly capsized the boat as he got on, causing Carmen to swear as she went below deck for a fresh glass.

"Dan," said Basil trying to keep his voice down. "I want Shelly, the new girl in Claims. It's only fair, you got Marcia."

"What!" screeched Carmen from the cabin; Basil who thought he had whispered was loud enough to be heard two boats away.

Carmen never said another word, instead of a wine glass she surfaced with the fire extinguisher and proceeded to hurl it at Dan.

The ex-Commodore of the Jamaica Yacht Club who was docked next to Dan was prostrate in his boat in a fit of laughter. Dan just missed being hit by the fire extinguisher by jumping into the Commodore's boat.

"You see what you cause in here today?" said an irate Dan from the relative safety of the neighboring boat, "Just remove yourself from my boat, I will deal with you tomorrow!"

And so began a day of misery that would also signal the beginning of the Pottinger's downfall.

Carmen threw her wine glass overboard and put the bottle to her head. Dan remained perched on the Commodore's boat and would not be brave enough to get back on his boat until the children returned for the journey home.

Dan sat up in bed and gazed at his sleeping wife. To get in so much trouble over Marcia was unfair, he thought. After three days in his employ he had decided that Marcia was too valuable to have a casual affair with. She was efficient and hardworking and had become his right hand and his left ear. The truth was there were days when he regretted his decision, but all the others he had slept with he had had to fire eventually and he did not want to lose Marcia. As quietly as he could, Dan eased himself off the bed and headed to the shower.

***

Elizabeth Ann Pottinger was dressed for school but instead of going downstairs for breakfast she was half way out the window to see a glimpse of her neighbor, Kevin Metcalf. What was it about this old man that attracted her so much, she wondered, as she watched him navigate his expensive SUV out of his driveway. When she could no longer see Kevin's car, Elizabeth gathered her books and headed to the kitchen.

"What in the hell happened here last night Lizzie?" asked Louise, as Elizabeth helped herself to juice. "Well," said Elizabeth, "as far as I can gather, Mom found out somehow that Dad is having an affair with Marcia Moore. Mom got pissed out of her brains and was last seen standing on the kitchen table stripping off her swim suit and asking Dad to look and see if she had any thing missing." Louise rolled her eyes as she prepared the coffee.

"Our ride is here Lizzie, step it up," said Bradley from the kitchen door.

"Have some juice, Bradley," said Louise. "No thanks Lou, at 2.30 this morning when they were still going at it, I came down here and made myself breakfast."

"So then mister next time you burn the bacon, please run a little water in the pan. It makes it easier to wash," Louise reprimanded gently as she watched the youngsters walk down the driveway.

Reluctant to resume her work, Louise lingered at the door way watching the children. She began working for their parents before they were born. Louise had fed and cared for Carmen during each pregnancy and the children were brought directly from the hospital and put straight in her arms. She had weathered many crises with the Pottingers and this one looked like it might be a big one. Louise returned to the kitchen and fortified herself with a cup of tea before the warring Pottingers arose.

As Louise stood at the kitchen window sipping tea, she could see all of Kingston spread below. The house high on Jacks Hill had a spectacular view of the Liguanea Plains on which Jamaica's capital city of Kingston sat. On a clear day Louise could count the container vessels that sailed in and out of Kingston harbor; sometimes she could make out the cranes on the wharf. The Pottingers bought this house five years ago when Dan Pottinger had taken over the insurance company. Louise fondly remembered the town house on Waterloo Avenue that had been home to the Pottingers for many years. Those were happy years. First of all, the house was way smaller and easier to clean and she never had a rass hill to climb every day. Love for the children and deep loyalty kept Louise climbing that hill, despite Percy's constant begging for her to stay home.

The move to Jacks Hill had brought changes that Louise would not have believed had she not seen them herself. Soon after the house, came the boat and then membership at the Yacht club, and if that was not enough, service clubs were added to the list. This was the beginning of their hard drinking and staying out late, leaving the children to their own devices. Unsupervised, the children were getting out of hand. Elizabeth's grades had dropped and Bradley, a computer wizard, had dark circles under his eyes at 14 from staying up all night on his computer. A bigger house meant that Mrs. Pottinger's mother, Doris, could now move in. Louise was not looking forward to this, it was rumored that Doris was showing early signs of Alzheimer's.

Dan entered the kitchen and Louise turned and looked him squarely in the face. "Good Morning Mr. Dan, will you please remove Miss Carmen's drawers from the fan and tell me what you want for breakfast."

"No breakfast Lou, just coffee, and listen, Miss Carmen is going to be in one of her moods today. Please do not let her fire you again." Dan moved quickly, mixing the biggest Bloody Mary Louise had ever seen. "Just give her this when she wakes up," he said, as he poured his coffee into a paper cup and beat a hasty retreat through the door.

Louise emptied the Bloody Mary down the drain, reheated the coffee and took the Panadol bottle out of the cupboard. She then prepared to heave her large frame up the stairs. She opened her employer's bedroom door without knocking, moving quickly and quietly to the bathroom. As expected, the bathtub was full of sand and draped with wet beach towels. Experience had taught Louise that if she wanted to escape a firing today, she had better get the Panadol and coffee down Carmen's throat as quickly as possible. With a tissue she cleaned the drool from Carmen's chin and gently shook her awake.

"My God you big black cow, what the hell are you doing?"

'Good morning to you too Miss Carmen," said Louise shoving the coffee and Panadol under Carmen's nose. "Here, drink this, you will feel better in no time."

"Who says I want to feel better, stupid bitch."

Carmen took the coffee and Panadol, but her expression belied her harsh words. There was a deep love and understanding between both women.

"Come Miss Carmen, get up and get in the shower. I will find something for you to wear."

***

'Oh God, I can't stand much more of this,' thought Carmen. She was dressed and sitting on the patio having a second cup of coffee and toast doused in Picapeppa sauce. Her too tight wig aggravated her headache so she tore it off and sat with her hair sticking on end in all directions. Carmen licked at the sauce running down her fingers. Picapeppa, a Jamaican sauce, was well known to cure hangovers. She needed to get away. When they moved to this lovely house she figured her life was settled.

Instead, the trappings of success were strangling her, choking her to death and her stupid husband was fucking around again.

She could go to her sister, Margaret, in Coral Springs. She loved her sister dearly. Her first instinct was always to run to her, but the last time she visited Coral Springs, Margaret had given her a colon cleanse, and made her drink seven kinds of green tea that had her shitting for a week. No, she did not have the energy for Margaret now, she would telephone her instead.

'Revenge is what I need,' she thought. 'Revenge, but how?' A smile spread across her face ...'Kevin Metcalf,' she thought. She had just begun to formulate a plan to gain Kevin Metcalf's attention, when Louise appeared on the patio.

"Miss Carmen," said Louise standing with arms across her wide abdomen. "Mr. Dan not having no affair, so do not fret yourself anymore."

"How do you know that Louise, how could you possibly know that?" Carmen asked.

"Well," said Louise, "his underpants are as clean as when he take them out of the drawer, no skid marks for years now, he drop them every day into the hamper fresh and clean. Not like that time when I had to soak them for a week before washing."

Carmen looked at Louise for a long time. Maybe she was clutching at straws but the band that had her chest in a vice grip all morning loosened and her head stopped throbbing.

"Thank you Louise," she whispered.

CHAPTER 2

Percy

Percy began pacing at five thirty. Mondays were hard on Louise and he had the Benjamin's healing oil ready for the nightly rubbing of the knees. Mondays she cooked chicken up at the Jacks Hill house and he knew she would bring a leg for him, so he had set on a pot of rice and some calalloo. At six he started to worry, she was sometimes late on a Monday but that did not stop him worrying. He turned off the stove and walked to the gate to meet her.

In the years since they had lived together, Percy had looked after Louise as best he could. They did not have much, except for the house that had taken him ten years to build, but he could afford to keep her at home. All his begging and pleading had not stopped her from going to her job every day. He waited at the gate. In the distance, Alton Ellis' 'Girl I've Got a Date' played. The song took him way back to 1966 when they had just come to Kingston. He stood and listened.

They had stepped off the bus at the Bus Terminus in down town Kingston, it was eight o'clock at night and a side walk sound system in front of the bus stop played rock steady music as loud as speakers in those days would allow. The bandage on Louise's head was now soaked through with blood and she looked like she was about to faint away. It had only been three days since her father Mass Ossie had beat her, so bad that she lost the baby. Mass Ossie had never liked Percy. When Louise told him she was pregnant with Percy's child, Mass Ossie flew into one of his rages. Luckily, Pastor Stoolie was passing by on the way to his farm and had slapped Mass Ossie across his back with his cutlass, stopping the old man from killing the girl. Percy was at sea with his uncle helping to haul in his fish pots.

Percy hated the sea. As he had leaned over the boat, he felt bile rise in his throat. He swallowed hard and prayed for a good haul, he needed the extra money. He knew Mass Ossie would be very upset at the news. Percy had started planning their getaway as soon as Louise had told him about the baby. He hoped he could keep himself from vomiting into Uncle Freddy's fish pot and silently prayed for dry land.

Percy had helped Louise down the bus steps, and felt terror grip his heart. He had very little money left after paying the bus fare. The cousin with whom he planned to stay until he got on his feet had no idea he was coming. She lived in Cross Roads and Percy had no idea where Cross Roads was.

Percy looked up from his revere and saw Louise hobbling down the road. 'Lawd,' he thought, 'the Benjamin's healing oil finish tonight.

***

Kevin Metcalf swung his SUV into the Jacks Hill driveway and glanced at the Pottinger's house, he was relieved to see all appeared calm. He was quiet, always clean and well dressed.

He was a very good looking man and hid his sixty two years well. Women loved him. He had learned to live with their admiration, always looking for ways to fend them off. He loved his wife, as much as he could love any woman, and was now conscious that she waited for him in the house, but he could not go inside until he had cruised the fence line for a glimpse of Denton.

All ten dogs started howling, the sound was awful, and it made Dan's blood run cold. He looked out the window in time to see Kevin Metcalf scampering away from the fence. 'Strange,' thought Dan, 'for an upstanding, first class lawyer, Kevin did some funny things,' but he did not dwell on it. He was relieved to come home and find Carmen in somewhat of a good mood, sober, and with her wig on straight. He had one hell of a day. First he had missed his meeting, then before he could sit down Basil had come rushing into the office....

"Dan before you kill me look at these figures," said Basil, turning on Dan's computer.

"The rumors are true. Everything will crash," continued Basil.

Dan looked at the computer with dread in his heart. He had gambled and lost. Foolishly, he had invested the company's capital along with his personal savings in an alternate investment scheme. Now his insurance company would fail the next minimum capital test and they would no longer be able to operate. More than half of the policy holders had defaulted on their premiums last month.

Dan forgot all about Basil's transgressions. The rest of the day was taken up with devising a plan to deal with the situation. The global economy was in recession and Jamaica was caught in the drain pipe. Dan had seen it coming but like most, had hoped their radars were malfunctioning.

Adjusting his stocking cap, Denton closed his room door quietly. He lived in what would have otherwise been the helper's quarters. The Jacks Hill house stood on over an acre of land which needed constant care, and when Louise refused to feed so many dogs the Pottingers reluctantly hired Denton full time to live in. Denton played the fool sometimes arranging his handsome face to look stupid, but he was no idiot. The house on Jacks Hill had become his refuge. He could sleep at night in safety away from the constant threats from the bad boys of Tivoli.

His grandmother had been a "follow Bustamante till I die," Labourite and he had been born and raised in Tivoli Gardens. He had barely learnt to read and write when his mother stopped him from going to school for his protection.

Early on Denton had identified with girls, he screamed at the top of his little lungs when he could not wear his sisters' panties. He wanted hair ribbons and clips so badly his mother would sometimes give in and put a clip or two in his hair. Needless to say this did not go well in the schoolyard. One day a mouse ran through the classroom and Denton screamed louder and longer than the girls. After that his fate was sealed, every mouse that lived in a five mile radius of school was put in Denton's desk, tied to his chair, put in his lunch and down his pants. Luckily Denton was a fast learner and had grasped the rudiments of reading and simple arithmetic because by grade five he was out of school.

Coming around the side of the house Denton was careful not to make a sound, he knew that Kevin Metcalf could be lurking in the bushes and he did not want to see him. Kevin Metcalf was talking foolishness about love and wanted favours for free. He was also a very dangerous man. Denton had been out twice with him to the clubs in New Kingston and was horrified at the people Kevin kept company with. He had also overheard two of Kevin's cell phone conversations which had made him very wary. Denton gave nothing away for free and his growing bank account proved it. He planned to go to California and had no time to waste on the likes of Kevin Metcalf. Denton was half way down the hill when his friend Claude picked him up. He got in the car, put on his wig and reached into his pocket for Carmen's newest lipstick.

***

Louise was in no mood to talk, so Percy helped her into her favourite house dress and fed her supper. He knew he would hear all about it when she felt like talking and did not press her for details. By the time the Benjamin's healing oil was finished Louise was fast asleep. Percy looked at her and thought he must try and find a foot to put down. She was exhausted and needed to stop hauling her ass up the hill every day. She was over sixty years old and needed to stop.

Percy went back to the gate to enjoy his last piece of cigar for the night. The strains of the old rock steady rhythm could still be heard. 'Man,' he thought, 'somebody riding the old riddims tonight,' and like earlier that evening, the music brought memories of 1966 flooding back.

1966 was a good time to be young in Jamaica. Things were not easy but there was hope. Four years after Jamaica gained her independence, people still had big dreams and plans for the country. Loads of young, rural people came to Kingston to find their fortunes. Back then everyone was hopeful, not like now, now that all those hopes and dreams had been dashed against the hard realities of black man time.

Jamaican music was coming into its own. Going to a frowzy rub-up at a dance on a Friday night was the best time. Dancing to the loud music of the sound system, holding Louise tight, tight and rocking. That was when music was music, he thought.

Finding six shillings to go to the Carib Theatre on a Saturday night had been a challenge but a reachable one. Today they could no longer afford to go to the movies.

Percy remembered the first time he saw the Carib. Tired and reeling from the long bus ride from Bluefields in Westmoreland, they had alighted at Parade in the heart of downtown. Percy asked for directions from a coconut vender who was packing up his load to go home. He had memorized his cousin's address, number 6B Pennrith Road. The coconut man gazed at the country bumpkins as if they were from outer space.

"Ok," said the coconut man, who was deciding whether to rob them or not, "take that bus on the corner, the one mark 35, ask the `ductor to let you off at the Cross Roads Terminus, and you will find Pennrith Road behind the Carib."

"Where and what is the Carib?" Percy asked. "No worries you not going to miss it."

By then Louise was about to collapse and the coconut man took pity on the girl and chopped a coconut for her to drink, which she gratefully shared with Percy. He also gave them a spice bun and a piece of dirty yellow cheese that he dug out from his shut pan.

The Carib was truly a spectacle. At the Cross Roads Terminus, Percy and Louise stood for a full ten minutes taking in the sight. The last show had just finished and people were pouring out of its doors in droves. Percy would have loved to stay longer but he knew he must find a bed for Louise. One more stop to ask directions and they were standing outside number 6B Pennrith Road.

"And just where are you going with that big old dirty gyal?" screamed cousin Maude. "You think you can just show up here Percy with a bleeding dirty gyal, you think this is a hotel?"

"Yes Miss Maude, please excuse me, I know I should have better manners, but when you hear the story you will understand." Maude was too tired to scream. She stepped aside and allowed them inside the small house. With Percy's help she made a cot for Louise. "You will have to sleep on the floor Percy, there is only one other bed and you cannot sleep with me, we not six anymore."

Louise was so glad to lie down that she did not care if Cousin Maude cursed all night. As she drifted off to sleep, she heard Maude asking Percy what the hell he planned to do with that big old dirty gyal.

Percy looked at Maude and thought that people always saw Louise's size first. Did they not see her majestic head, her full mouth with the straight row of strong white teeth? Her soulful eyes were large and almond shaped with the pupils as black as night. Could they not see her long shapely legs and her splendid backside? Louise's cool black skin was so soft that Percy wanted to put his face in her neck and stay there. She was his girl and he would love her forever.

Percy turned away from the gate, he hoped that Louise had not sprawled herself across the bed. Most nights he had to find a small space and hang on for dear life.

CHAPTER 3

Doris

Doris Morrison arrived the next day.

"Mother what the hell!" Carmen exclaimed. "Didn't I tell you I would send for you at the end of the month?"

"Yes."

"Then why didn't you wait?"

"Because you are a fucking liar."

"Mama!" Carmen screamed, unaccustomed to her mother using such words.

"Clifford told me to come."

"Mama, Clifford is dead."

"No, he is not!"

"He is Mama, ok, then tell me where he is?"

"He lives under my bed ..."

Carmen stood on the patio staring at her mother her mouth wide open. 'Could she have deteriorated so quickly?' she thought. It was only three months to the day that Margaret and Carmen had been summoned by old Doc Martin and told about their mother's condition, but she had been given pills to slow the Alzheimer's. "Mother have you been taking your medication?" A now frightened Carmen asked.

"I don't need medication, nothing is wrong with me. I give all the pills to Clifford, he is dead, and he needs the pills."

Clifford had been Doris's husband on and off for fifty years and Margaret and Carmen's father. Although Clifford came and went as he pleased, sometimes disappearing for months at a time, there had never been any talk of other children. Clifford died five years ago while eating banana porridge; having suffered a stroke months before. He had come home for good just in time to get sick and die.

Doris had a stiff upper lip and endured all her troubles with Clifford with a smile and not a hair out of place. She was also a cleanliness freak. Once on one of her visits to Carmen, Louise had found Doris on her knees inspecting the underneath of a chest of drawers with a flashlight. When Louise inquired of the old lady what she was doing, Doris calmly told her she was looking for dirt.

"Mama, where are the pills?" asked Carmen who was now on her knees opening Doris's suit case. "Mama, you know how much those pills cost!"

"Yes dear, but the pills are not wasted, I give them to Clifford every-day," said Doris.

"Mama, where are your panties and your nighties? I only see dresses in this suitcase."

"Oh Carmen, don't you know that panties are Babylon? Don't you know that panties are useless pieces of claat used to keep us in bondage?"

"Free up yourself girl!" screamed Doris as she lifted her skirt above her head.

Louise watching and listening from the dining room was doubled over in laughter, she knew it was wrong but she could not help herself When she thought just how proper Mrs. Morrison had always been and to see her now exposing her skinny ass for the world to see was too much for Louise.

"Mama," said Carmen, "we need to talk!"

"Talk to yourself Carmen, I'm hungry, I haven't eaten anything all day. Where is that big gyal that cook the food so good?"

"Bigga!" shouted Doris, "I am hungry!"

"Lawd see it ya now, tek the case," mumbled Louise through tears of laughter.

Still on the floor repacking the case, Carmen wondered if Clifford had somehow caused the onset of this most dreadful disease. Doris had suffered silently through the abuse that Clifford had metered out, always making excuses for him to the girls. Doris made up stories about Clifford's travelling for work, and the girls were fooled for a number of years, because he would turn up at regular intervals. Clifford had been a good provider and Doris had never been forced to work and had occupied her time getting her hair and nails done. She went out of her way to court anyone she thought had social merit. She wrangled invitations to all the best parties and functions, and in time she became a regular on every party list and as a result, part of the scenery. This lifestyle worked for them all, the girls did not mind having a part time father. He turned up in time to pay the bills and that was important to them. Until, Sally.

Sally was a half Indian girl from Maggoty and half Clifford's age. Clifford must have been hopelessly in love with her because he gave her everything. He bought Sally a shop and stocked it with goods. He built her a house which she promptly filled with all her relatives. Doris, Carmen and Margaret saw less and less of Clifford and less and less of his money. For years, Clifford was in heaven, he had a young beautiful girl and all her relatives' dancing attendance in return for a few dollars. After a while Sally's shop started to do well. She had paid close attention to all of Clifford's business dealings and learnt to manage herself and the shop. Inevitably, one day Clifford arrived home to find all his belongings moved out of Sally's room. When he enquired, Sally told him that his farting and snoring at night in his sleep had gotten on her nerves. She had to work long hours every day in the shop and could no longer be kept awake by all that ungodly snoring.

"Also," said Sally with hips akimbo, "get some carbolic soap Clifford, you are smelling like a real old man."

At this time Doris spent more time at the window watching and waiting for any sign of Clifford. She had grown silent and morose, and her stiff upper lip was crumbling. The girls had married and left home, and she was glad when Clifford returned with his tail between his legs. Unfortunately, Clifford missed Sally and the house full of relatives, within weeks of returning home he had a stroke and that was the end of that.

Carmen could not wait for Dan to come home. For some reason, Doris was always on her best behavior when he was around. Carmen called his cell phone but it went to voice mail. Much as she hated to, she called the office line. Marcia Moore answered and told Carmen that Dan was in a meeting.

"Meeting!" screeched Carmen. "Girl if Dan is not on the phone within ten seconds, I am coming down there."

"Ok, Mrs. Pottinger, please hold on."

'Shit,' thought Carmen. 'Clean drawers, clean drawers… maybe next time I won't shout at her.'

"Carmen," said Dan, in his 'this had better be good' voice.

"Dan, Mama is here and she mad to rass. I am at my wits end. What the hell am I going to do?"

"First of all, what is she doing there already? I thought we were to pick her up at the end of the month?" Dan asked.

"Well she told me Clifford sent her."

"Listen Carmen," said Dan, getting annoyed. "Please do not call and provoke me. The dollar gone to 88 today and now is not the time for this. I am going to hang up, I will talk to you later, give your Mother a pill or something".

Carmen sighed and put down the phone. If Clifford had left some money all this could have been avoided. Everything had been left for Sally, however, and there was not a damn thing Carmen could do about it. Doris had gone to live with her cousin who was a cantankerous old witch and that situation would come to blows sooner or later, so it's just as well she was here now.

CHAPTER 4

Extra Work

It took only two weeks for the extra work to start telling on Louise. Doris was a handful and Louise had to press Denton into service more and more. Denton did not mind as he got to wear his soft slippers in the house, and had more time to go through Carmen's things, smell all her perfumes and try on her wigs.

Louise had realized that she had not paid enough attention to Denton. What she had mistaken for backwardness was an act Denton had put on to hide what he really was about. Now that they were working closely together, Louise saw flashes of intelligence and realized that Denton was cunning and smart. Denton was the only one who could get Doris to take her medication. Her blood pressure medication could be disguised in her food but the pills for her Alzheimer's had to be swallowed. He cajoled, sang and danced and distracted her sufficiently for her to swallow the pills. This exercise took two hours of his day and on some days his work got behind. This morning he had to get out his hose and attend to the dog shit in the yard.

It was a breezy morning and the smell of dog shit permeated the house.

In the mean-time, Louise was busy cleaning Doris's room; Carmen was hurrying to get dressed. She had to get her goods today. Doris had taken up a lot of her time on doctor's appointments, blood tests and so on. She was behind in her business and feeling more than a little anxious. No one saw Doris slip through the back door. Doris had been restless all morning, her mouth was hurting and she was looking everywhere for Clifford.

Carmen had just taken up her car keys when she heard the blood curdling scream coming from the Metcalf's, she got to the back door in time to see Denton scaling the fence. She knew that she could not scale the fence and got in her van and drove over to the Metcalf's as fast as she could. Carmen was just in time to see Alice, the Metcalf's helper, fanning Shirley Metcalf with a copy of the Daily Gleaner.

"What happened?" asked Carmen, out of breath. "That!" said Alice, pointing to the table on which sat a glass of orange juice with Doris's false teeth floating in it.

Apparently, Shirley was sitting on the patio reading the newspaper and having a late breakfast when Doris, who had wandered off looking for Clifford, had walked in unnoticed and dropped her teeth in Shirley's glass. Shirley, whose head was buried deep in the newspaper, looked up, reached for her juice and saw a full set of dentures grinning at her. Shirley recoiled in horror as her chair toppled to the ground.

Carmen apologized profusely and grabbed the teeth out of the glass and shoved them in her mother's mouth. Shirley quickly regained her composure and told Carmen not to worry.

"I have been meaning to invite you over for ages," Shirley continued, "but Kevin does not like to entertain."

"That's ok, we can get together soon," said Carmen. It was the first time she had seen Shirley up close and was surprised to find her so pretty.

Leaving Denton in charge of Doris, Carmen rushed back to her van.

As soon as Carmen's heartbeat had returned to normal, her cell phone rang. It was her friend Joan Silvera reminding her that she was hosting a committee meeting of the Kiwi Club in two days. Normally Carmen enjoyed hosting meetings, but now with Doris in the house, she did not know how she was going to pull it off.

"Shit Joan, all the drama with Mama, I just plum forgot about the meeting," said Carmen, thinking of all the work involved. "Would you be able to do it, Joan?"

"No darling, much too busy, but if I shift some things around I may be able to help you. So tell me who else did you invite to sit on this committee?"

"Well," said Carmen trying to remember, 'Circle Food', Chatty Cathy, Scatter Teeth, 'Thousand Teeth', Miss High and Mighty, Lucy Goosie, Call me Pearlie, 'Tight Bun' Betty, and loud mouth Gertrude."

"Listen to me Carmen, you have got to stop doing that," said Joan giggling. "One day you are going to slip and call some-body one of those names to their face."

"Well I can't worry about that now, I am already so late and I will have to stop and get a case of wine. I will talk to you later, bring you up to speed with Mama and you can help me plan the god damn meeting."

Carmen rang off and carefully backed her minivan out of the Metcalf's driveway. She was late for her appointment with her customs broker, who had cleared her latest shipment.

Joan Silvera and Carmen met in high school and went to university together. Carmen left after her first degree and Joan stayed to do her masters' degree. Joan was currently doing research for a chemical company while Carmen had taught high school until leaving the Waterloo Avenue house. Carmen loved teaching and while the children were younger the hours and holidays suited her, but she needed extra income to furnish the Jacks Hill house and had begun selling wigs on the side. The business did so well she was able to leave teaching behind. Now she was one of the largest importers of all things false. False hair, false nails, false bottoms, false breasts, girdles, body shapers and a line of large handbags.

Joan was responsible for her joining the Kiwi Club. Normally a lowly teacher would never have been invited to join. In this chapter of the Kiwi Club one had to be a lawyer, doctor or Indian chief to be thought eligible to join. These ladies were absolute snobs when it came to profession and place in society. Also, you needed money. Dues were high but that was only the start, hosting a meeting, paying fines and finding clothes to wear to all the activities could run into a tidy sum, not to mention the copious amounts of liquor sucked down at these gatherings. The club did a lot of good in the community, and the ladies were a fun loving bunch, but the social and networking sides were just as important as their good works. Apparently, these ladies did not know that the Lord said you were to do your good works in secret. They were fond of giving each other plaques and citations and hosted countless meetings in honour of each other. They were never happier than when their pictures appeared in the daily newspaper. Carmen got into the club and held her own simply because her merchandise appealed to them so much. Last week 'chatty chatty Cathy' needed filler for a pair of pants that did not fit well. In no time, Carmen got her a girdle with enough padding sewn in to fill out her bottom. 'Circle Food' was good for at least one body shaper and two handbags each month, and 'Thousand Teeth' bought enough tooth whitener to keep the entire club's teeth white for years.

Stanley Newman, Carmen's customs broker, was pacing impatiently when she finally got to his office. Carmen was nervous as she had overextended herself. This was her largest shipment to date and Stanley was breathing down her neck back for his cheque, wanting as usual payment in full. Carmen needing a little wiggle room had asked if he would wait until she had sold some stock and accept a half payment now. Stanley paced some more before answering. He was an officious little tight ass and never gave credit, but he liked Carmen a lot and did not want to lose her business.

"Yes Carmen, ok, but I expect three quarters and not half payment, and the last quarter at the end of the month". Agreeing quickly, Carmen wrote the cheque as fast as she could. She fled his office before he changed his mind, leaving him still agitated and pulling at the wedgie in his pants. By the time she made another stop to pay for the transportation of the goods, she was very short on cash, so when she got to the liquor store to buy a case of wine she reached for Dan's credit card. While waiting for the wine to be loaded into her van and the card to go through, Carmen made a cell phone call home, but before she got an answer she was interrupted by the clerk to say Dan's card was declined.

****

Carmen did not scream at Dan the way she typically would at the shame of having the credit card declined. She had taken to smelling his boxers at night and was pleased with every fragrant whiff. Instead of screaming she hurriedly fixed his favourite rum and coke and waited at the door. She saw his stressed expression and clearing her throat to remove the whine from her voice, asked if he knew why the credit card was declined.

"Don't use the card again Carmen," said Dan with downcast eyes. "I can't pay the bill; in fact I won't be able to pay any bills any time soon."

Carmen's head felt hot and prickly under her wig she fidgeted in her chair trying to understand what Dan had told her. She knew instinctively that he was not joking and groped around in her mind to find words.

"We are fighting like hell to keep the office open, Basil is working day and night to keep us afloat," continued Dan, "and I have lost all our investments, every cent of the money we worked so hard to save."

Carmen could not get her voice to work, her head got so hot that she took off her wig and scratched her head. She had heard rumours about the alternate investment scheme going sour, but dismissed it as just a rumour but here was Dan confirming her worst nightmare.

"But you are not screwing Marcia Moore!" screeched Carmen suddenly finding her voice.

"What the hell does that mean Carmen?" asked Dan. "What has that got to do with anything?"

"That means," said Carmen, "that we can start again Dan, go back to the basics, get rid of some of the trappings, and the first thing we are going to do is sell the boat."

CHAPTER 5

The Meeting

Elizabeth Pottinger was not pleased to have her grandmother in her house. She had never liked Doris and if anything, she liked her better crazy. When she was a little girl she always plaited Elizabeth's hair too tight and insisted Elizabeth be dressed in socks even on the hottest days. Elizabeth remembered the headaches she endured until she was able to persuade Louise to redo her hair. Doris had never been an affectionate grandmother and it was difficult for Elizabeth to love her. Today, because of the meeting her mother had asked Elizabeth to keep an eye on Doris, Elizabeth had reluctantly agreed.

Elizabeth did not like the meetings either. Carmen always found chores for her to do and by the end of the evening her mouth hurt from smiling with the old biddies. Doris who had been relatively calm all day became excited and agitated when she saw the food.

Elizabeth toyed with the idea of locking Doris in her bedroom but quickly decided against it, she would probably scream her head off.

"Grandma go and sit on the step, I will get you some cake and we will watch the ladies arrive," said Elizabeth trying to calm her grandmother.

"I want the whole cake, you hear girl I want the whole brown cake," Doris said, hopping from one foot to another.

"Ok Grandma," said Elizabeth. "If I take the whole cake we have to go upstairs so Mom won't see."

"Ok, Ok, Ok, just get the god damn fucking cake!" said Doris almost foaming at the mouth.

By the time the first guest had arrived, Elizabeth and Doris were comfortably seated at the top of the stairs where they could view the proceedings and hide the chocolate cake.

Joan was the first to arrive looking chic and cool in a pale green linen suit, leaving a scented trail of Jadore in her wake. Elizabeth admired Joan and wondered why she put up with her mother's madness. Next came 'loud mouth Gertrude' and as she passed them Elizabeth thought she must use an entire tube of lipstick every day to cover those enormous lips.

The rest of the ladies seemed to arrive all at once and things became noisy as Denton started serving the wine. Most of the ladies were matronly, powdered down, and squeezed into out-fits far too young for them. Her mother's wigs and false nails were prominent and as the room got warm and the wine flowed there was much patting of faces with large wads of paper towels to keep their makeup from running into their ample bosoms.

Elizabeth had just decided that Doris had had enough cake when Gertrude loudly announced, "The President is coming! The President is coming!!" Her announcement was followed by a hush as all the ladies stood at attention for the arrival of the President.

"The President is coming!" screamed Doris, her mouth full of chocolate cake. She then let out the loudest fart Elizabeth had ever heard.

Joan was the first to start giggling and by the time 'Tight Bun' Betty' the President got to the door the whole room was screaming with laughter. It took Carmen fifteen minutes to call the meeting to order and by that time half a case of wine was consumed and none of the ladies seemed interested in the meeting any more. 'Circle Food' took the opportunity of their distraction to fill her handbag with sandwiches and cake. Carmen watched her out of the corner of her eye, but said nothing, 'Circle would need a new handbag soon.'

The Kiwi Club had many rituals, and introductions were a big part of any meeting. If a member had held an office in the club it was never forgotten.

... "This is call-me-Pearlie, immediate past President most effervescent, Lord of the Rings, Lady of the Manor and so on" ...

By the time they got to the business part of the meeting, most of the ladies were not thinking straight and Carmen decided to send them home while most could still drive. At the last meeting at Gertrude's house 'Thousand Teeth' took off a section of the gate post and crashed into a fire hydrant and, Carmen, worried about finances, wanted to save a few bottles of wine.

Drunk on chocolate cake and full of gas Doris nodded off. Elizabeth got Bradley to help her cart Doris to bed then went to help Denton and her mother clean up. Dan had avoided the crowd and slipped through the back door and into his study. Elizabeth was concerned and conscious of the change in her father's demeanor. She had overheard part of her parents' discussion about money and although worried, she had no idea at the level of shit that was about to hit the fan.

Feeling proud having helped her mother, Elizabeth went to her room and locked her door. After checking her bedroom window for signs of Kevin Metcalf she sat at her computer and went through her emails. She had two addresses, one she used to send secret messages anonymously to Kevin. She checked to see if he had replied. He had not, so she opened a new email and wrote.

I want to see a picture of your penis.

She pressed send and went to bed.

Carmen made the rounds checking that all the grill gates were padlocked then went to the kitchen to make a cup of tea. Denton had left the kitchen spotless. He wanted to spare Louise the extra work tomorrow. Sitting at the kitchen table sipping tea, Carmen knew she had just hosted her last meeting of the Kiwi Club. She would have to find an excuse to leave or just stop going to the meetings. Either way she was pleased to find that instead of feeling sad she felt light headed with relief. Her only concern was that she might lose some of them as clients. With the exception of Joan she would not miss them, especially 'Thousand Teeth' who had started looking at Dan as if she would suck him through a straw.

*****

Marcia Moore struggled to get the pot out of the bottom drawer of her desk. She had been late that morning and had no time to put the rice and peas in a Tupperware container. Marcia had started taking food to work when lunch was not enough to satisfy her growing appetite. She had put on quite a bit of weight but she did not care, she had a bag of number eleven mangoes in her car and she was going home to eat every one.

Dan's friend, Dunstan Watson, had taken to bringing her gifts of mangoes and if his tree did not stop bearing soon, she was going to explode.

The tension in the office was affecting her and she was no longer sure she could cope. She found that she was hungry all the time and noticed that for the last two weeks she was getting up in the middle of the night to eat.

Marcia had tried everything she could think of, short skirts, low cut blouses, expensive perfumes, hairstyles of every description, hair up, hair down. She had spent a fortune on new makeup but all her efforts were in vain. Dan Pottinger had not given her one un–business-like glance. She had fallen head over heels in love with him by her second day of work and it was killing her to see what was happening to the firm and the effect it was having on him. So love sick and unhappy was she that she had not given much thought of what she would do when the firm finally closed. Reaching down to slam the desk drawer she felt her panty hose give way reminding her that she needed to stop at the dressmaker to collect the clothes she had given to be let out.

Marcia had taken to confiding in Dunstan Watson. The old commodore came to the office regularly and they had struck up a friendship centered on Dan and their concern for him. She called Dunstan at least three times a day to lament the state of affairs at the office. She had become very fond of the old man who spoke slowly and smelled of cigarettes.

****

"Sell the boat!" exclaimed the ex-commodore. "Man you out of your rass mind. You of all people should know that you would have to give it away. I do not know anybody who would pay full price for it now, even if they had the money they could beat down your price!"

Dan had driven out to the Yacht Club seeking the old commodore's advice. Dunstan Watson was retired and could be found most days sitting on his boat. Dan respected the old man who had been his sounding board on a number of matters.

"But Dunstan, you are not listening to me, any money would be welcomed now, the bailiff came for Carmen's minivan this morning and ICV is about to foreclose on the house. I cannot believe how fast this melt-down is happening. Carmen is able to keep us in groceries and pay the help at home but not much else."

"Dan, this is one time I do not have any ready answers for you boy," said the old commodore, as he backed off his Top Siders and hung his feet over the side of his boat. "All of today I have been thinking that I will have to come out of retirement. When I stopped working the money I had put aside looked adequate enough, but inflation licking it out faster than you can say who kill cock robin."

There was a long pause while both men were lost in thought. Finally, Dunstan said, "I have a house in Mona Heights, just locked up. I cannot stand the tenants any longer, they just mash up the place. You and the family can move in if you do not sort out this foreclosure."

"Thank you Dunstan," said Dan thinking about Louise, Doris, Denton and the ten dogs in a Mona house. "It is very comforting to have a backup plan, but I am thinking I may have one more option."

"Good," said Dunstan. "You take your time and think about it." The two men sat a while longer, Dan trying to erase the Mona Heights picture from his mind and Dunstan thinking about Marcia Moore's ever growing backside.

Louise and Denton knew something was not right in the house. Louise was certain she had sorted out the other woman business with Carmen. She was puzzled about the continued long faces everyone was wearing. Doris was causing less trouble and regular taking of her medication had calmed her a lot. Denton, encouraged by Louise, had started listening at Carmen's bedroom door and outside Dan's study but was unable to learn anything. Not until this morning when they came for Carmen's minivan that both of them looked at each other in the kitchen and blurted, "Money Worries!!!" In unison, "I have some!"

"Stop it!" said Denton, cutting Louise short. "You not going give away you and Percy's money just so. Let us wait and see what is happening, nobody tell us anything yet."

"How did you know I was going to say money?" asked Louise, wiping her hands in her apron. "I had to study you good Louise. From the first day I come here, I know that if I don't get into your good books, I don't stay here. So I know you was going to say money," he declared.

"But if we could only find a way to help them," said Louise, close to tears. "Don't worry," said Denton. "You think I waste my time when I leave here at night?"

"Listen boy!" said Louise. "Don't chat any foolishness in here this day and cross my spirit, I spend all day trying to not think about what you are doing at night."

"All right Miss Louise, I have an idea. Let us discuss it with Mass Percy."

"Yes," said Louise, "is the first intelligent thing you said all morning."

There had been a series of robberies along Jacks Hill Road. Men on motor bikes were holding up household staff on their way home and Denton started to escort Louise to the bus stop and wait with her until she was safely on the bus. Once he had followed her all the way home and met Percy. Even though Louise had told Percy all about Denton, Percy had backed himself into the corner of his small verandah; it had taken four white rums to get him out. By the end of the visit, Percy and Denton were chatting and laughing like old friends. Denton was looking forward to seeing Percy again. Not only did he enjoy his company, he was sure that Percy would be able to help in thinking through his plan.

As Denton and Louise started down the road, they could see Percy swinging on the gate. "Lawd Jesus him drunk," said Louise. "But I don't understand that. It's not Friday. What him doing drunk on a Thursday?"

"Him drink all the time Miss Louise?" asked Denton

"No Denton, only sometimes on a Friday he will have a que or two with his friend Joseph. They get a little stupid, but swinging on the gate look to me like a major drunk."

As they got closer Denton could see the white rum flask sticking out of Percy's pocket and the end of a cigar in his mouth.

"Percy what the hell you doing?" asked Louise, with obvious annoyance in her voice. "It's not Friday!"

"I know it's not Friday, you think I am stupid. I am celebrating," said Percy, climbing down unsteadily from the gate.

"What the hell are you celebrating Percy?" asked Louise. "I come home early to talk some serious business with you today and I am very vexed to find you in this condition."

"Well," replied Percy, "they cut me down to three days a week instead of five, cut my pay too."

"So is that a reason to celebrate?" asked Denton puzzled.

"Yes Denton, they lay off fifteen people today at least I have three days."

"Well you had better sober up fast; we need to talk to you. I may not have my job very soon unless we can think of something," said Louise, pointing Percy in the direction of the house.

"Stop, stop," said Percy standing his ground. "I am not listening to one god damn thing unless one of you buy me some more white rum and another cigar."

Without another word, Denton set off through the gate. Louise was able to pilot Percy into his favorite chair on the verandah.

"Greed," said Percy, waving the new bottle of white rum. "Is greedy them greedy, that is what causing all the trouble in the country. Nobody satisfy with what them have. Too much fish head eat in this country that is why we can't get anywhere and is not only the Politicians. Jamaican people on the whole just greedy."

"What is fish head?" asked Denton.

"Do not encourage the stupid argument," said Louise.

`Well it's like this," said Percy, ignoring her. "A contractor gets a road to build. First of all he has to pay the politician a percentage of the money before he can get the contract. That is fish head. In my younger days, it was just about ten percent. Back then, quite a few white men were still around so they did have a little conscience. But today, it may be fifty percent for all I know. Then the contractor licks out the other half. So when the people start to block the road because it still full of pot holes, the contractor run and throw down two pebbles and some marl, throw some black tar on top, make two or three runs with a roller and baps, new road. The first time the rain fall after that almost every piece of new road wash away."

Using the pause in Percy's rant, Denton said, "Percy, we have some problems."

"Wait!" bellowed Percy, stopping again to light his cigar. "I not finished yet."

"You see the new highway?" continued Percy. "Rain fall, breeze blow, chicken batty out a door and not even one pothole. You know why?"

"No," said Louise and Denton.

"Because the foreign people come down here and build it. They put the righted amount of stone, the righted amount of marl and roll the road tight. I never knew that a road could build in Jamaica without it mash up after rain. And you see what happen now? Ole niggar have to pay money to run up and down our very own countryside!"

"And what is your point Percy?" asked Louise her eyes glazing over.

"My point is this my dear, the road works is just the start of the worries. That fish head greed run right through everything in this country. Road is just the example I am giving you. If things was running right, the contractor get his job without having to pay fish head. He might be inclined to do right by the road and give his workers a fair share. Then the roads would last a little longer, taxi man would not have to buy so many tires, spend plenty money fixing front end on the cars so he might keep his fares down. The market people could get their goods to market easier so more food would grow. Parents would have a little ease with the bus fare so can give the children some more lunch money...the children then might learn a little more... you see Louise? If things was running right, I would have my rightful five days a week work instead of three!"

"Amen," said Louise. "But you know well that it is not as simple as that, bad things happening everywhere."

"Yes but we could be in a better position to stand up to it," said Percy.

"Well!" said Denton. "My night business fall off, not many customers lately. The girls doing better than us though."

"Why are the girls doing better?" asked Percy.

"Because batty more expensive than pussy!" said Denton with a straight face.

Before Louise could react to Denton, a volley of gun shots rang out into the night.

"Get inside quickly," Louise hissed at the two men. Louise locked the door and instructed Denton and Percy to keep away from the windows.

"The war start again," said Percy. "I hope it does not last as long this time."

Gang warfare was a regular occurrence in the neighborhood and Louise and Percy were accustomed to lying low every so often until things cooled down, but Denton was terrified. The house was hot and airless having been locked up all day and as beads of perspiration rolled off Denton's face. He asked Louise, "How the hell am I going to get out of here tonight?"

"I am not letting you out of this house until day light, so relax and let us fix a little supper."

Louise and Denton went to the kitchen to fix supper and Percy fell into a white rum stupor, snoring loudly as his head rested on his chest. He awoke with a start when they came back,

"Louise" he announced loudly. "You can give them the land in Bluefield's."

"What Percy?"

"I said you can give them the land. I know what you two come here today to talk to about, and the only thing I can do is give Miss Carmen the land!"

"How you know about what is happening Percy?" asked Denton. "You a mind reader now?"

"No," said Percy, "only sometimes I can read Louise. But seriously, remember my friend Joseph, that work at JPS? He told me last week that for three weeks now he have Miss Carmen house to disconnect and every day he cross it off the list. He say if he don't stop, them going to fire him."

"Percy, I know you hate the sea but you well know that one day I want to go back to Bluefield's to live. I want to throw my old body in the sea twice a day. Dip hairy mango and guinep in the sea water and eat fish every day."

"Louise, is me you talking to you know?" Percy unscrewed the white rum bottle. "Look how many years I begging and pleading with you to leave the kill dead work up the hill and now you are telling me about relax? Eh? I know that if you were serious, we buy the hairy mango and gone a country long time."

"Wait, wait a minute. Woah!" Denton exclaimed. "A little land down in God forsaken Bluefield's not going help Mr. Dan too much. But before we get to that, please, tell me how you and Miss Louise get land."

"Well since you cannot leave here tonight and I have one of my many days off tomorrow, I going tell you the story," Percy lit his cigar.

"Percy, do not smoke that stinking thing in here!" shot Louise.

"I can't go outside, so cork you nose Louise!"

"You think is only black man capture land, Denton?" Percy quipped.

"Of course, is only black man I know steal land!"

Heh heh," Percy chuckled. "I was about ten when Busha Morgan ride into Bluefield's in his Land Rover. You know the old time Land Rover that rattle like tin can? He pull up to the shop where my father and Uncle Freddy was playing dominoes and said he needed some chaps to do some work. Well, the sea was rough so Papa and Uncle Freddy never had much to do, so them jump into the back of the Land Rover and ride off with Busha. Two days later Busha drop them back at the shop. Papa said that they measure out and peg over five hundred acre of land and that Busha was coming back in two days to start fence it. Uncle Freddy never want any part of Busha and his fence work, but Papa said the money was good so he would work with him for a while. Papa said the fish would still be in the sea when he got back. Well Papa never get back to the sea, cause Busha fence up the land, plant sugar cane, graze over two hundred head of cattle and had a pig pen with over three hundred pigs. About five years pass and one day Busha brush down his blonde hair, put on his Busha hat and ride into Sav-la-mar tax office."

He say, "I've come to pay my taxes," to the clerk in the office.

The poor girl reply, "But Sir I have no property tax notices for you,"

"In those days," continued Percy, "you don't question white man, when a white man tell you to do something you do it."

"There must be some mistake, call your supervisor," Busha told the girl.

"Well Denton, to cut a long story short, Busha leave Sav-la-mar with five years notices and five years receipts. Some more years pass and one day Busha dress up himself again, this time he got a brand new Land Rover and no hair on his head. So he brush down the little fringe of puss hair left on his head back, put on his Busha hat and ride off into Kingston. Well you must know what happen now?" Percy asked.

"No," said Denton who was sitting up in his chair and enjoying the story. The gunshots outside forgotten. "Come on man, tell me the rest," urged Denton.

"Busha went all the way to Constant Spring Tax Office, open up him two blue eye at the tax man up there and tell him, "I come for me Title!"

"NO!" Denton was incredulous.

"Yes!" laughed Percy. "As easy as that, Busha tief nearly five hundred acre of Crown Land!"

"So what else happen?" asked Denton.

"This time Busha had to pay some money and it took three days, but he came back to Bluefield's with his title. At that time we never know what was going on. Papa continue to work for Busha until he got sick bad, and when Papa got sick, all Busha had for him were three small words....Sorry to hear!!!."

"If it was not for Uncle Freddy, we starve to death. That is why even though I hate the sea so much and nearly vomit out me tripe a dozen times, I always had to help out Uncle Freddy. Because of the way Busha treat Papa I never put my foot back on Busha farm, so when I got the telegram to say that Busha dead and leave me ten acres of it I nearly wee wee up miself."

"Ten acre, rass Percy, is a whole heap of land that! But I still don't think is enough to help out Mr. Dan. Percy, look, Louise fall asleep."

"Can see that you love her, don't it Denton?"

Denton replied, "Yes Percy, where I come from woman rule, man come like ghost and shadow. I grow with some strong woman; only woman like them could protect a beeps man in Tivoli."

"We never had any children after Mass Ossie beat out the one we got; we never got any more again. I know she love you like those two children up at Jacks Hill."

"So you have a title for the land Percy?" Denton wondered.

"Yes. Busha fix up a nice title for me with my name Percival Jonathan Grant." Percy beamed.

"I think you should keep your land. I want to see Miss Louise get to dip her guineps and hairy mango in the sea water. Percy, she is always talking about that you know, does it really make the fruit taste better?"

"It look so, Denton. One day when she was young, I got her a big Jack Fruit and she and the Jack Fruit stay in the sea the whole day."

"Anyway Percy, I have a plan, but is a dangerous plan and it could backfire if we not careful. This is why I come here tonight. I want to talk to you about it. I need you to listen carefully and trouble-shoot it if you can."

"Troubleshoot!! Rahtid, Denton you not easy, Louise know about it Denton?"

"Not all the details, she would try and talk me out of it if I told her everything. Just listen Percy, Louise ever tell you about a man name Kevin Metcalf?"

CHAPTER 6

The Plan

"SHIT!" screamed Carmen. Shit was her favorite word these days. Denton was on his way upstairs to help Louise give Doris her bath and had peeped on Carmen who had just finished on the telephone. C&L had disconnected their land line; the Pottingers was down to two cell phones.

"What happen Miss Carmen?" asked Denton.

"Call Louise and the both of you come here," said Carmen, "and look in the study, see if Mr. Dan left any cigarettes in there," instructed Carmen.

"I am not having a bath now. I just had a bath, my pussy is not dirty!" screamed Doris from upstairs. "But you not smelling so good Miss Doris." Louise was tired from chasing Doris around the bed. "Just a quick little wash Miss Doris. Elizabeth going to vex with me if I do not bathe you today."

"I don't care who vex with you. I am not going into the bath today. I never slept with no man last night so I do not need to wash anything."

"Leave her Louise," said Denton from the door way. "Miss Carmen want to see us now on the porch."

Turning to Doris, Denton patted her on her head and said, "Never mind you hear Miss Doris, when I am done with Miss Carmen I am going to come for you and we will go outside and play with the garden hose."

***

"I am going to tell Mr. Dan on you Miss Carmen. What you doing with the cigarette?" said Louise, as she fanned the smoke.

"Just ignore her Miss Carmen. She lilli bit miserable today." Denton making himself comfortable on the floor at Carmen's feet.

"Come and sit too Louise."

"No Ma, you and Percy out to kill me with second hand smoke." Louise kept her usual stance, legs wide and arms folded over her belly.

"Ok listen. I know that you know what is going on here. We are having serious money worries. Mr. Dan has a plan; he is trying to get another company to merge with his to get us out of the worries. Do you understand so far?"

"Yes Miss Carmen," they said in unison.

"And another thing," she continued, "we lost all our savings so we have nothing to fall back on. Plus I foolishly overextended myself and bought too much and things aren't selling so well. We have two to three weeks at the most to stay in this house and Margaret who does not know what is happening just phoned to say she and her husband are coming to visit. It will be their twenty fifth anniversary and they want to have a party here. What

I want to know is, can we somehow pull a party together on a shoe string budget plus hide what is happening from Margaret?"

"No problem Miss Carmen." Denton's mind was already working a plan. "If you give me some girdles I can get a good price from my boys. I did tief one the other day and we try it on. It keep in the pump and tool kit very well and give a nice shape to the important parts. That's the liquor money right there."

"Lawd God!" bawled Louise.

"Hush you mouth Louise," said Carmen, already counting the money.

"What else, Denton?"

"Well, I know where I can get some meat kind and my friend Claude can help serve and Percy can help Louise cook."

"But you know how Margaret stay; she won't be contented with just chickens, she going want beef and ham." Carmen was warming to the plan.

"What I want to know is why Miss Margaret can't pay for her own party? And where we going in two to three weeks?" demanded Louise, as she rocked from side to side looking unhappy.

"Mona Heights. Dan has a friend who will lend us a place in Mona Heights."

"Mona Heights!" screeched Denton

"I can't work in Mona Heights, Miss Carmen. No decent upstanding yard technician work in Mona Heights! I not going able to hold my head up on the Strip. We going come up with a plan for the party and we going to stay right here. I not moving."

"You still have not answered my question Miss Carmen," Louise was still fanning cigarette smoke.

"You damn well know Louise, when we go to Margaret, we are treated like royalty. We are taken to restaurants, every night, and feted and petted. Miss Margaret is not going to spend one penny in this house, over my dead body!" Carmen blew smoke at Louise's face.

"Miss Carmen, don't worry yourself no more. I will have everything under control before tomorrow night, just give me the girdles and we can cover the liquor. I know where we can get a pig and I have a little money to buy some chickens. We going have BBQ chicken and suckling pig," Denton gushed. "How much time so we have and how many people?" he asked.

"Margaret will email the list tonight but I figure at least 50 people. By the time we count up family it will be almost 30. She wants to see some of the Kiwi members, the ones she knew before she left. So today is Tuesday, Margaret comes on Friday and the party will be Saturday night."

"Not a problem Miss Carmen, leave it to Louise and me," Denton assured her.

"The way I see it, I have no choice," her eyes glazed by her anxiety.

*****

"Me first!" screamed Denton standing on the back lawn, with the dog shit hose going full blast.

"No, no, me first!" said Doris grinning like a little girl in anticipation of the game.

"Ok then," said Denton and turned the dog shit hose on Miss Doris soaking her from head to foot.

"Bring the soap now Louise!" shouted Denton.

Together they tenderly bathed and dressed Doris, right there on the back lawn.

CHAPTER 7

Pat and Sheila

Dan stretched his legs, leaned back in his chair and closed his eyes. He had exhausted almost every avenue available to him. He figured at least 10 million dollars would keep the wolves at bay for another week to give him time to see if the merger would be approved. He had his doubts and was preparing staff for the eventual shut down. He was tired, he hadn't slept well for a week and he felt the fatigue wash over him. Marcia quietly placed a cup of coffee on his desk. He would be sorry to see her go, his heart warmed at her loyalty and support and that shown him by the entire staff. Even Basil had turned out to be not such a bad chap after all.

There was nothing more he could do here today except to pray for ten million dollars to fall through the ceiling. He packed his desk and called out to Marcia, "Please call Mr. Watson and tell him I will be stopping by the club to have a drink with him."

"Dunstan!" Marcia started to cry.

"What now my love…," he whispered.

"Dunstan you loss you mind, why are you calling me my love?" Marcia retorted, forgetting her tears.

"If I am not your love why you calling me every day? Every evening you disturb my nap. I am an old man now you know. I need my rest," Dunstan bristled.

"All right, keep your clothes on. Dan say he stopping by the club to have a drink with you this evening."

"So is that anything to cry about?" he asked.

"I think we will have to close the office next week," she began crying again. "I don't know what I am going to do, how I going to pay my rent and eat?"

"Don't worry, I will look after you. I will feed you number eleven mango until I have to roll you in flour to find the wet spot."

"You know Dunstan you getting rude, very rude," said Marcia as she hung up the phone.

Dunstan closed his cell phone and heaved himself off the bunk and prepared for the walk to the club house for more ice. The refrigerator on his boat just did not make enough. He paused to gaze at the water from the boat's deck. He had a splendid view of the Warika Hills and he could see the smoke curling from the chimney at the Cement Company.

Dunstan loved this time of day, the sun was setting and the sea breeze was dying in preparation for the land breeze that would come later. Unfortunately, this was also sand fly time.

Dunstan hated to go home, his wife Delores was home. For the life of him, he could not remember why he married her. Delores was a meager woman whose bones jutted out at all angles.

Dunstan kept his dark glasses on sometimes just to look at her. When he married her, she had had meat on her bones. She was normal until the birth of their second daughter Kitty. When Kitty was born, Delores decided she had to lose the baby fat and had gone on a diet and had never come off. The last time they had sex, which was some years ago, Dunstan had insisted she keep on her clothes. As one would imagine, it did not go down well with her.

Delores was an incessant chatterer. She talked as soon as she awoke until she went to bed. Many mornings Dunstan awoke to find Delores perched on his side of the bed waiting for his eyes to open to start chatting. The only rest he got was when she was on the telephone. He was the only person he knew with a telephone bill higher than the electricity bill.

The girls discovered early that a book in front of their faces was the only way to derail their mother's chatter. As a result, both girls did very well in school and escaped the house as fast as their scholarships could take them.

Food was her other contention, Del had been on every diet known, he had endured the cabbage diet, the lemonade diet and other diets too numerous to mention. Now she was only eating green things, callaloo, string beans, and okras was her latest daily menu. He had stopped eating at home years ago. Thinking of food, maybe Dan would have dinner with him at the club house tonight, he was tired of dining with the bartender.

*****

Denton was about to go on his nightly run when he paused to listen at the living room window. He heard Dan tell Carmen he was not hungry and had eaten at the club with Dunstan. A loud psssst interrupted Denton. Across the lawn he saw Kevin's wave. Signaling him, Denton returned his attention to Dan and Carmen's conversation.

"If I could only sell the boat," moaned Dan, "it could buy us time."

'That's it,' thought Denton. 'That is it.'

Excited by his plan, he crossed the lawn to speak with Kevin.

"What happen rude boy?" purred Kevin in his sweetest voice.

"Kevin!" called his wife, Shirley from their house.

"Oh golly, that damn woman," he grumbled.

"Don't worry darling," Denton consoled. "I not going to the strip tonight, but have a little business to do now, so bathe and powder till I get back."

***

Denton linked with Claude at the foot of Jacks Hill Road.

"You wicked you know, Claude, you could drive up the hill for me."

"Buns of steel boy, buns of steel," said Claude. "You must walk, how you going keep your steel buns if you don't walk? Where we going tonight?" he asked.

"Denham Town," said Denton.

Claude stopped the car at the Loshusan Corner. "Get out the car now, I not in no madness tonight."

"Drive the car boy before I tump out you claat," Denton warned. .

"Ok, ok, just don't lick mi!" Claude conceded, "where exactly we going in Denham Town?"

'Elgin Street."

"Lawd God Denton, no, tell me we not going to Mr. Herman house? Remember how fraid of Mass Herman we are? What we going do at Mr. Herman?" said Claude visibly shaken.

"We going to tief one of Mass Herman pigs," declared Denton,

"NO, no, no, no!" Claude protested, "I don't want to go anywhere near Mass Herman house much less tief him pig."

"If you think I won't beat you to a pulp tonight, try me." Denton kept an eye on the road as Claude's driving was taking a turn for the worse.

****

Herman George Edwards was an old and ugly white man fallen on hard times. His wife and children had left him in Denham town years ago and migrated to the United States. He was a Three Card and Crown and Anchor Man and he delighted in terrorizing the neighborhood children and most of the adults too.

"Why can't we just buy a pig?"

"Because we have to buy the chickens and the rice and the vegetables. Rass you think I am a millionaire?"

"Denton," said Claude, "you know how pig shit stink, if the pig ever shit in the car I going kill you."

****

Jerry Hughes stood in the dark in his back yard pissing on his callaloo patch. He was Mass Herman's neighbour and arch enemy. They had quarreled for years about the odour of Mass Herman's pig pen. Each time Jerry had called the authorities to remove the pigs, a new fight broke out. Mass Herman only had two pigs now but Jerry could still smell the stink of the pen.

Satisfied that most of the callaloo had received his blessing, Jerry was about to move when he saw a car backing in close to the fence. Curious, he stopped to watch. He saw two men alight and stealthily climb the fence into Mass Herman's yard.

'Please, dear God, let it be the pigs they come for,' Jerry thought.

Last night he could not sleep. The damn things squealed all night.

As the men came alongside his fence Jerry said, "Wait."

Claude, already terrorized, jumped near out of his shoes, but Denton turned to the familiar voice," Mass Jerry?"

"Yes is me, who dat Denton?"

"Yes sah, is me."

"You have to take the two of them," said Jerry to Denton.

"How you know I come to take anything?" Denton asked.

"I look like a fool to you? Listen up, if you don't move fast Herman going to hear, and if you don't take the two pigs, I going talk. You follow?"

"Yes, Mass Jerry."

"Ok, take these," Jerry pulled up two freshly wetted stalks of callaloo. "Give these to the pigs, if they are eating they won't make so much noise, wait on me, I am going to get Bella to stand watch." Jerry ran to his window to summon his wife.

"Bella, hurry to the front and stand guard for Herman."

"You gone mad Jerry, I have on me nightie, what you want me watch for mad man Herman for?" she asked.

'Them come to steal the pigs Bella; don't let him come to this side of the yard."

"And how you expect me to stop Herman if him decide to come?" she asked, not unwilling to help but wary.

"I don't know Bella, think of something, let you titty drop out of you nightie or something," said Jerry, anxious to get the pigs in the car.

"Ok," she said jumping out of the bed, always ready for a little slackness.

"Yes boys, let's go." Jerry grabbed some more callaloo just in case.

It was easy enough getting the pigs out of the pen and trotted to the fence with the callaloo bait but getting them over the fence and into the car was another story. The pigs were not big but quite heavy and they started squealing loudly as Jerry and Denton stuffed them into the back of the car.

From a deep, sweet, white rum induced sleep, Herman heard the pigs. He was reluctant to get up; at first he thought Jerry's puss had gotten into the pen again. That man Jerry kept that puss just to provoke his pigs. By the time he realized the noise was not coming from the pen but the fence, he heard the slamming of car doors and the pigs squealed no more. Fighting the white rum haze he fought to clear his head and by the time he got to the door, he saw the tail lights of a car as it sped off down Elgin Street.

"Whoa." Claude was shaking at the ordeal. "Never again you get me to do that."

Denton did not answer. He was fighting to keep the pigs from ripping up the back seat. They were squealing and rutting around, trying to escape the moving vehicle. They had only reached Collie Smith Drive, when Claude screamed, "Turn around and sit down quick. Denton Police!"

"What?" Denton turned around and strapped himself in quickly.

Claude struggled to compose himself and drive slowly by the squad car parked on the corner, but no luck tonight. The Sergeant waved them to pull over. By some miracle, the pigs stopped rutting around as the car stopped.

"Let me see your papers."

"Oink, oink, oink," said a pig in the back seat.

"What the hell!" exclaimed the sergeant. "You have pigs in the back? Corporal bring the big flashlight."

"So you are praedial larcenists?"

"No, not at all commissioner," said Denton. "These are my pets, this one name Pat and that one is Sheila."

"Oh yes, really?" The Sergeant quipped, "And what are you doing with your pets in the car at this time of the night?"

"Well sir, we taking them for a drive," said Denton.

"Really now, why?" The Corporal shone the big flashlight on the pigs.

"Them can't sleep," said Denton.

The Sergeant could not control himself, he began to laugh and soon they were all laughing.

"Tell me the truth and I may go easy on you, where you get these pigs?"

"Them belong to Mr. Herman sir."

"Mr. Herman Edwards from Elgin Street?"

"Yes sir, same one," said Denton, thinking about Denham Town Police Station.

"Where are you taking the pigs?"

"Jacks Hill Road sir. We going to cook them for a party."

"Corpie load up, get in the car and turn on the blue lights, we going escort Pat and Sheila to Jacks Hill Road."

"Eh?" Denton grunted in shock.

"Yes," said Sarge, "long time we want to get rid of them pigs."

CHAPTER 8

Poor Louise

Carmen could not believe it but the worse things got, the better she felt. She must be some kind of psychotic bitch. She put away her wigs and yesterday had gotten her hair cut short; leaving a sprinkling of grey and her natural curls. This morning she scrubbed her face and did not apply makeup. Dressed in comfortable jeans and sensible sandals, she bounced down the staircase ready to start the deep clean in preparation for Margaret.

The house had to be spotless and smelling like a rose for Margaret's visit. She wanted Margaret to feel the same way she felt when she visited her sister. Making a mental list of tasks she thought about the Coral Springs house. Words could not do justice to the feeling one had on entering Margaret's house. It was like entering a cool, safe sanctuary. An escape from the harsh realities of this world; the aroma, ambient lighting and Margaret knowing what you needed before you had thought of it. The only thing to be avoided in Margaret's house was the colon cleanse. Margaret believed a dirty colon was the root of all evil. If your head or back hurt, or toenails needed cutting, Margaret said, "Poisons in the system, must cleanse."

Otherwise, a visit to her home was the most relaxing time one could want. Carmen always left Margaret's refreshed and happy, and she was going to make damn sure Margaret was well looked after, with or without money.

Carmen found everyone congregated at the kitchen window.

"What's outside?" she asked.

"Come look Mom." Bradley gave up his space at the window.

"Oh my God!" she laughed. "I did not know that dogs and pigs could play together! Did you get them for a good price Denton?"

"Yes ma'am an excellent price. I arranged with the butcher down at the supermarket to come later and deal with them. He even gave me bottom price too," he said with a broad and knowing grin.

"Right, everybody out of my kitchen, I have plenty to do today," said Louise waving her tea towel.

Elizabeth and Bradley were suspicious and uneasy with recent events in the house and had volunteered to help with the cleaning and party preparations. They had taken a new interest in their mother, who had suddenly found some time for them.

"Found the paint mom," called Bradley.

They planned to paint the carport area and verandah wall soiled by the dogs. .

"I am just not sure how much water we need to stretch it."

"Let's see." Dan had come in to get his coffee for the office.

"Here Dad," said Bradley. But Dan did not look in the paint pan. He was staring at Carmen as if he had not seen her for years. He walked around Bradley and whispered in her ear, "Welcome back girlie," then put his mouth over her cheek and gently sucked on her face.

This sent shock waves down to Carmen's very toes. For a moment, the universe was centered on her husband's mouth.

"PDA! PDA!" shouted Bradley bringing Carmen abruptly back to earth.

"Let's go," said Elizabeth.

As she covered the walls with watered down paint, Carmen reflected on so many years of piling mountains of stress upon herself. A bigger house, expensive cars, club dues, the boat, cocktail parties, luncheons, all so they could keep up with the Jones', the Browns, and the Smiths of this world. They wasted time away from the children, and lost hours in drunken stupor.

'And for what,' she wondered. Now all she could think of was getting through the week. If she was lucky, at the end of all this, she would be in a double bed somewhere in Mona Heights with her husband sucking on her face.

****

Shirley Metcalf was fascinated at the sight of dogs cavorting with pigs on the Pottinger's back lawn. She called to Kevin to come see, but he was singing and splashing in the shower.

'Why was he in such a good mood this morning?' she wondered. He could not have had much sleep last night. She had awoken at 3:00 am and he was not in the bed. She never worried; he was prone to wonder the house at all hours of night. Usually he would be tired after these excursions.

This morning he was happy and making quite a racket in the bathroom.

"Kevin, why are pigs on the lawn next door?" she asked Kevin who was out of the shower and admiring himself in the mirror.

"Oh, I meant to tell you, we are invited to a party over there on Saturday night, they are going to roast the pigs."

"Oh yes, well there is a dog trying to mount one of the pigs over there," sniffed Shirley. "Are we going to eat that?"

"Come away from the window Princess, maybe you should think of buying a new dress for the party."

"I have a dozen dresses I haven't yet worn Kevin, you never take me anywhere."

It was true. Kevin treated Shirley like a porcelain doll.

For a long time she was flattered that a man like Kevin Metcalf wanted her locked away for himself, but lately she had been wondering.

"So how come you taking me to this party?" asked Shirley, but Kevin was no longer listening. He was thinking about last night, reveling in sweet memories. One thing bothered him. A couple of flashes from Denton's cell phone. Kevin was no fool, he knew he was about to be blackmailed, but he had been in that place many times before. A simpleton yard man would not pose much of a problem.

****

Louise felt heavy in her chest. She knew she should rest but there was too much to do. She was doing as much advance food preparation as possible. She was stirring barbeque sauce on the stove. She had started with two bottles of store bought to which she added ketchup, picapeppa and an entire bottle of hot sauce. Everything today was about stretching, Miss Carmen watered down the paint and now she was stretching the sauce. The extra pig was a God send; they had not been able to buy as many chickens as hoped. Percy had accompanied her to the farmer's market early that morning and was now scrubbing potatoes for the potato salad.

Denton brought his friend Claude to help. He looked fairly normal and Louise didn't mind him, especially because he had a car and he transported the heavy market basket up the hill for her.

Claude was now arguing with Denton in the kitchen.

'We have to put it in all of them?" said Claude.

"No," Denton insisted. "Suppose Elizabeth or Bradley or heaven forbid, Miss Doris, eat one? No I don't agree."

"What you talking about?" Louise was still stirring the sauce.

"We have a special ingredient for the salt fish fritters, but we only want the people who going drink out the liquor to eat it," explained Denton. "Only the men."

"So what when one of the ladies ask for a fancy wine and we don't have it?" asked Claude.

"No problem." He went on, "two salt fish fritters then we give her rum straight up in a wine glass and she won't know the difference," answering himself.

"You know the draw-back to that don't you?" asked Percy from the sink.

"Yes, them going eat more food, but we will have more food than liquor, don't worry Percy, leave this to the experts."

"I don't want to know," said Louise.

The dogs frenzied barking deafened Denton as he let in another friend to help them decorate and serve at party time. Claude had appointed himself bartender and head cook and bottle washer.

"Miss Louise please put on the kettle, Denton gone for Lipton and he going to want a cup of tea as soon as he come back; this dude Lipton grow in England and all he do all day is drink tea, that's why we call him Lipton."

"Yikes," Percy yelped when Lipton appeared at the kitchen door and blinked twice at the spectacle that was Lipton.

"Ello mates!" he called. "Can we have a cup of tea before we start?"

"I tell you Miss Lou," Claude retorted.

Percy stared at Lipton's full head of bright yellow hair, the same colour as the Allamandahs in the garden. He had a bushy, black mustache, one diamond looking knob in one ear and a dangling earring in the other. Dressed all in white and in a pair of pink shoes, he smelled of Johnson's baby powder and Wrigley's chewing gum.

"Did you get the flowers?" he asked.

"Not enough money," Denton replied.

"You mean you tief two whole a pig and couldn't tief a few flowers?" asked Lipton incredulously. Slamming his tea cup on a table he exclaimed, "Look here boy I didn't come here to waste my time you know. I am going to the garden to see what I can find, in the meantime get me all the Christmas decorations and lights in this house."

The dogs barking resumed, in a minute Lipton was back, "somebody come and call off these bloodhounds. I think the butcher is at the gate, so you need to see about that too, and let me tell you all something else...I not running down no pig."

****

Louise made herself a cup of tea and sat at the kitchen table. She could not understand why she felt so tired. She had been doing a lot of extra work but nothing to warrant this exhaustion. Everything that could be done beforehand was done. The chickens were prepared and seasoned, in plastic bags in the refrigerator, the sauce was made, the peas for the rice was soaking, salad greens washed and bagged and also in the refrigerator. The potatoes for the salad were cooling. Only thing left to do today, thanks to Denton and his friends, was to cook the stewed peas and rice for dinner tonight. It was Miss Margaret's favourite, and she cooked it every time she came to visit.

'Might as well start,' Louise muttered and began to stand but half way up she felt the first pain. It felt like a heated knife was plunged deep in her chest. "Whoa...," she groaned, as the pain rocked her back in the chair. She rested her head on the table as she rode out the pain; it was a pain that made you feel as if it would take you away. It left her as quickly as it came. She sat thinking, this is not good, something must be very wrong but she needed to help with the party. She would ask for time off to go to the doctor, after. She finally heaved her bulk out of the chair and started dinner.

Dan came home some time later. He and Carmen planned to meet Margaret and Lester at the airport. He stepped onto the freshly painted patio, Lipton was busy decorating a column with flowers and lights, and in the dining room Denton was feeding Doris and encouraging her in a soothing baby talk. In the living room Claude was rearranging the bar. Dan met Carmen on the stairs.

"What is going on?" He exclaimed, "Are we having a party or a battyman Jamboree?"

"Shh, please Dan, I do not want to hear you talk like that. I could not have done any of this without Denton and his friends.

"I understand that Denton is now part of this family but not sure I can manage the one with the yellow hair!" said Dan. "Are you ready?"

***

As the car drove away, Denton ran for the dog shit hose. The Butcher had taken care of the pigs and they were gone for the night to the supermarket refrigerator. The pigs had left little piles of shit all over the yard; mixed with the dog shit it was creating an unbearable smell. He had to clean up and lock up the dogs before Miss Margaret got here. He was rolling up the hose when he saw the orange electricity provider vehicle stop at the gate. 'What now,' he thought, abandoning the hose and heading to the gate.

"I have to do it tonight," said Joseph. "I have to disconnect tonight."

"Mr. Joseph?"

"You know mi boy?"

"Yes, you are Mr. Percy friend."

"Mr. Joseph I know you can disconnect the meter but leave the feed to the house. We having a party tomorrow and I don't think we can get away with candlelight. You can come back on Sunday or Monday and disconnect?" pleaded Denton.

Before Joseph could respond there was heart rending shout from Percy, "Denton come here now, something happen to Louise!"

Joseph and Denton raced up the driveway, colliding as they rushed through the kitchen door. Louise was sprawled across the kitchen table and Percy was hanging on trying to prevent her falling to the floor.

"Get some aspirins in her mouth!" said Doris. The alarm in Percy's voice seemed to have shocked her into a lucid moment. "She is having an angina or a heart attack, get her to a doctor now." She exited the kitchen as quickly as she had come.

The pain subsided and Louise righted herself and sat up in the kitchen chair. She swallowed the aspirin Denton gave her and said, "Yes, I need a doctor this is one bad ass pain."

"Claude gone with the car, let me call and get him back," said Denton.

"No that's going to take too long we will take her in the JPS truck. Look like we are all going to get fired anyway so no matter, we can all go to Bluefield's and plait sand and stone breeze,"   said Joseph.

"We are not taking her to any public hospital, over my dead body!" said Denton as they lumbered down Jacks Hill Road in the Jamaica Public Service truck.

"We have no choice, we have no money," said Joseph. "University might take her without money."

"How you feeling now Louise?" asked Percy.

"Just very tired," she said, "in between, I feel ok but when the pain come Percy its awful." Louise replied with tears in her eyes.

"Don't cry Louise, please!" he pleaded, himself close to tears.

"You know I can't stand it when you cry."

"Ok, ok we soon reach now," said Joseph, driving the old truck as fast as he could through Hope Pastures.

"Call Cousin Maude for me, tell her, no ask her if she will work for me up the hill tomorrow," instructed Louise.

"Don't talk Miss Lou, just rest," said Denton.

"Remember you have to dig the holes and get the coals going for the pigs by nine in the morning," she continued. "The pigs will take all day to cook. If they go in the ground too late we are going be in trouble."

The sound of the truck bearing down on the casualty door of the University hospital awoke the guard with such a start he nearly fell off his chair. Joseph jumped out of the truck and told the others to wait while he got help.

"Hey you!" said the guard to Joseph. "You can't leave the truck parked there."

"Did I ask you any questions?" shot Joseph.

"No," said the guard.

"Well shut your god damn mouth," Joseph marched on.

The hospital odour hit Joseph as he entered, 'too late to back out now,' he thought.

The room was filled with an assortment of people sitting on benches apparently waiting to be seen by a doctor, but there was no sign of a doctor or nurse anywhere.

"Do you know where the doctor is?" Joseph asked a lady seated nearest to him.

"Somewhere down that passage, but things going very slow tonight only one doctor," she said.

"It's always just one doctor," said the man sitting beside her. "Cho, I just tired of them."

"Look, I don't have any time to wait," said Joseph and set off down the passage.

In the truck Percy was comforting Louise. "Joseph watch too much ER, I bet he thinking some doctor and nurse going fly through the door with stretcher and the bag drip. Come you hear Louise, take your time and climb down out the truck, let we go inside."

By the time they got to the door, out came Joseph holding an orderly by the scruff of his neck.

"This is the lady." Joseph released his death grip on the bewildered orderly.

"Well," said the orderly arranging his shirt and pants back on his body.

"We don't have any stretcher that will carry her, she will pop down all the ones we have in here. The only one we have that would fit her, them steal off the wheels to make Go-Cart, cool runnings!"

Joseph growled and the orderly quickly continued, "So we can take her straight into an exam room."

As soon as they got Louise settled on an examination table, Denton slipped outside and called Carmen. He reported all that had happened and promised to call again when Louise was seen by the doctor. Carmen told him three flights were landed and they were still waiting on Margaret and Lester to clear customs, and promised to check in at the hospital on their way home.

Back inside, Percy was falling to pieces and shaking uncontrollably. "You won't be any help to Louise if you don't pull yourself together," said Denton.

"Ok, I will try," he promised.

"Leave the man alone Denton!" Louise barked from her bed. "Is not every day a man wife dead."

"Stop it! Stop it!" said Joseph, as a nurse entered the cubicle.

"Please, all of you leave, I need to get her vitals and somebody has to do the paper work," she said.

"I don't know who and you going get me to leave," said Percy.

"You the baby father?" asked the nurse.

"No, I am her husband," he said through gritted teeth.

"More like the baby grandfather," sneakered Joseph.

"Didn't I tell you to leave!" she snapped, as she strapped on the blood pressure cuff and shoved a thermometer in Louise's mouth.

No one moved, no one said a word, as the nurse pumped the pressure cuff once, twice, three times. Suddenly she dropped the pressure ball and without removing the cuff, ran from the room.

They were still speechless when nurse returned with the doctor in tow. She shooed them all out of the cubicle. This time they left quietly and stood in the waiting room.

Joseph went to park the truck after the guard threatened to call the police. He was forced to park on the other side of the hospital compound; on the long walk back to the casualty, he wondered why he had never found his own Louise.

He had watched the love between Percy and Louise for years and lamented on why it had eluded him. Joseph was a quiet, thoughtful man, not given to excesses. He had tried on many occasions to settle with one woman but it had never worked. His last woman tried to pour hot oil in his earhole one night while he slept because he had been talking to a young girl on King Street. After that, he had not wanted any women in his house. To spend a night, maybe, but come morning they were put out, toothbrush and all.

He had a year left to retirement and had worked at the Jamaica Public Service for forty years. He hoped he had not jeopardized his pension for stealing the truck. No matter, he thought, he still had his National Insurance, and now and then his son Joe sent a hundred dollars from New York, he had no dependents and so could help his friend Percy.

"Louise had a heart attack," Denton announced as soon as Joseph walked in the door.

"They not even moving her tonight as the doctor thinks she is in danger of having another one. Miss Carmen is here now, so she and Miss Margaret talking to the doctor."

"Boy, what a night," said Joseph collapsing into a chair.

"What are we going to do now Denton?" he asked.

"We have to pick up Miss Maude at Cross Roads, then go by Louise house and pick up her things, then back here to give them to Percy then up the hill. You in, or should I wake up Claude?"

"No, I will do it," said Joseph.

"Thank you man, I really didn't want to wake up Claude, we need a fresh body in the morning to dig the pig holes. As I see it, we have a long night ahead of us," said Denton.

" I will just go tell Miss Carmen that we have to go."

 On the walk back to the truck, Joseph asked Denton why they needed to bring things back to the hospital.

"You never have anybody in the hospital Joseph?" asked Denton.

"No," said Joseph, "never."

"Not even a baby mother?"

"Yes, I had two but I give them taxi fare," he said proudly.

"Lawd Jesus! Joseph, no wonder all of them leave you rass."

"So what do we have to bring back?" asked Joseph again.

"Nighties for Louise, towels and soap and the usual cosmetics. Then we have to bring a pillow for Percy so he can sleep in the chair, because you know he not leaving her. We have to bring him some coffee in a Thermos and something to eat. He is not hungry now but he will be."

"First stop, Maude," said Denton, as they climbed back into the truck.

"That woman have an evil eye and a mouth to match," moaned Joseph.

"I never meet her, I only hear Louise mention her once or twice. Percy spoke to her. She should be ready and waiting for us."

"She is Percy's cousin, I meet up with her all the time at their house but I just keep out of her way." Denton hardly heard him, he was very tired from all the work he had done that day, plus he was sleep deprived from the night of the pig run and all the romping with Kevin after. The gentle rocking of the truck and the drone of Joseph's voice put Denton into a deep sleep.

"So you the batty boy Louise love so much?" shouted Maude,

Denton abruptly awakened. They were parked in front of a little wooden house on Penrith Road. Joseph was helping Maude get into the truck.

"Let him sleep Maude," said Joseph. "He have a long day tomorrow and the night not over yet."

"Oh yes, well as long as him understand that I not like Louise, I am not a condoner of slackness. She opened her heart to all sort of things, no wonder it attacked her."

Denton, too tired to argue, smiled and drifted off to sleep again.

Thankfully, Maude kept her mouth shut until they arrived at Louise and Percy's house.

"I know where everything is," she said. "It will not take too long to put things together, I just need one of you to take down the suitcase off the wardrobe and put on the kettle to fix the coffee."

Maude was a small woman half Louise's size. It was impossible to guess at her age, her small face was smooth and unlined. She was agile and with lighting speed found towels, night clothes, and added items like Louise's Bible and healing oil to the suitcase.

Louise and Maude had been good friends for years. Once she had gotten over the shock of Percy dumping Louise on her doorstep, cousin Maude took another look at Louise in the light of day. Upon awakening, Louise had felt better, and had flashed Maude one of her brilliant smiles and Maude had fallen under her spell.

Percy and Louise lived with Maude for nine months. Maude taught Louise to cook and everything she had learned about housekeeping. By the time Louise left Maude's tutelage she could make a bed with the precision of hospital corners, set the table, prepare a tea tray, knew the basics of meal planning, shopping and keeping a bathroom so clean that your employer would think you had cleaned it every day. On that day when Louise left, Maude had cried like a baby.

Denton did not awaken as Joseph and Maude packed the suitcase and plastic bags stuffed with Percy's pillow and blanket in the truck. Joseph had tried to talk Maude out of taking the blanket, but she had insisted that the hospital was near to the hills and Percy would be cold. A flask of coffee and some guava jelly and cheese sandwiches would be good enough. Joseph, not a young man, began to feel the effects of the day as he maneuvered the big orange truck out of the lane and in the direction of up town.

CHAPTER 9

Lester and Margaret

Carmen sat heavily on the bench in the casualty ward of the hospital. There was no getting around it she knew she had to tell her sister what was going on. Carmen shifted uneasily on the hard seat. She was surprised at the depth of her fright at the thought of losing Louise. Louise needed an injection that cost in excess of a hundred thousand Jamaican dollars. Carmen knew she had to get it for her friend. She beckoned Margaret to sit beside her and without consulting Dan, launched into her story.

Halfway through Margaret stopped Carmen long enough to tell Lester to arrange for payment for the injection.

"Carmen, I am hurt that you felt you could not take me into your confidence. However, what is done is done. We will cancel the party, it's not important at all," Margaret determined.

"No Margaret," said Dan, standing nearby listening. "I invited one of the big wigs from ICW so I could entertain him. I know it was wrong to piggyback on your party, but I need to speak to him, our entire future rides on this merger."

"Ok," Margaret conceded, "what can I do now to help?"

"Nothing right now, Denton has arranged everything." Carmen answered.

"You left all the party arrangements to the gardener boy? Have you lost your mind?" asked Margaret, her voice raised. .

Carmen had no answer, she was so afraid for her friend Louise and all she cared about now was that Louise got that injection.

"You guys go home I will wait until Louise is settled for the night. I don't want to leave her until she is out of danger,' said Carmen.

"No, we are not leaving you here, we will all wait," said Dan firmly.

****

Lester was a happy man. Little worried him he could always see the funny side of everything. He had an infectious laugh and always somehow convinced others to do his bidding. However he had drawn on every resource he had, to deal with the sour faced woman at the hospital's cashier window.

"I never see a credit card like that," said the old biddy.

"Listen sweetheart," said Lester, "just slide it in the machine, it will work, I promise you."

"Huh?" she eyed the card suspiciously and adjusted the carbon paper in her book.

"I need an ID," was her next request. Lester took out his Florida driver's license and slid it under the window.

"So how you expect to get a TRN number from that?" she asked, sticking her pen in her hair.

"Listen darling, just try the credit card, if the payment is approved, you are sure to get the money," said Lester, growing impatient.

"You look like an oily mouth man. I need a TRN number to track you down."

"Well I do not live here anymore, I do not have a TRN or whatever and I need to make this payment, a lady's life is ticking away as we speak and if you don't run this card now I am coming around there and I am going to squeeze those big breasts of yours until you bawl like a cow!"

"Security, security!" she bawled.

The guard was fast asleep but the doctor came running.

"Listen doc, I can't get this lady to accept my valid American Express card, and that is the only way we can pay for Mrs. Grant's injection."

Bent in half from exhaustion, Doctor Campbell looked at the card and instructed the sour faced girl to run it. He waited until the approval slip emerged from the machine then hurried to administer Louise's injection.

****

Louise felt the sting of the injection and opened her eyes. She had been having a dream. She looked across at Percy who was sitting bolt upright in the chair and smiled at him. From a far-away place she heard the Doctor tell her to uncross her legs to not hamper the blood flow to her heart. She promptly fell asleep again. Louise had been dreaming about her father, she was six years old and her father had carried her on his shoulders to the sea. The water was clear and warm and Louise felt safe and protected on to her father's neck as he swam out to deeper water.

Oswald was slow, he was a slow learner but he was so big and appeared so normal that it was seldom recognized. He was often called ignorant. Many times through the years Louise had tried to mend the rift between them but Ossie stubbornly refused to speak to her.

Finally in 1992, her half-brother, who she hardly knew, sent her a telegram to say Oswald was sick. Louise got to Bluefield's two days before he died and had made peace with the old man. For the first time, Louise understood that the look on her father's face was not anger but confusion.

****

Dan stopped the car in the middle of the driveway. Carmen, Margaret and Lester got out and Dan joined them as they all stood with mouths open at the spectacle before them. The entire front of the house was covered in lights. White sheets and palm fronds sprayed silver had transformed the porch. Their carport had been made into a fairy tale wonderland with Carmen's five boxes of Christmas decorations sprayed silver and used to tie the look together.

Margaret was the first to recover.

"The gardener boy did this?" she asked Carmen.

"One of his pals, Lipton, and you will meet another of his friends, Claude, who will tend bar," answered Carmen.

"This is really lovely, but where are the tables and chairs going to go?"

"Our budget could not cover rented tables and chairs, so we opted to use the little money we had after we paid for food and liquor to use for decorations and go with a cocktail party theme, sometimes it makes for a better party."

With no help to unload the car, the four tired adults heaved and hauled Margaret's four heavy suitcases inside the house where they found Lipton, Elizabeth and Bradley making white paper lanterns at the dining table.

"There are no more tea bags," said Lipton annoyed. "I am sleeping here tonight so I can be up early to finish, and I am useless without my tea."

"Oh, but the place looks lovely," gushed Carmen. "What more is there to do?"

"I have to light the bushes along the driveway, duh," said Lipton incredulously.

"Well I will borrow some tea bags in the morning from Shirley Metcalf, I am sure she will have some until I can get to the store."

"You know," continued Carmen as she turned to her sister, "we have lived in this house for years and I only met Shirley Metcalf recently and we know none of the other neighbors."

"Yes I noticed that on my last visit," said Margaret, "very unlike Jamaica. Remember the Waterloo Avenue neighborhood parties?"

"Yes," said Carmen. "I think we are lost, we have lost our way, it's not too late though, and I am going to make sure we find our way back. Come on let's heat up the stew peas and rice."

****

No one stopped Maude, Denton and Joseph from going in to see Louise and Percy. It was now two in the morning and all was quiet. Percy was extremely happy to get some food and wrapped himself in the blanket just as Maude said he would.

Maude placed a silent kiss on Louise's forehead and squeezed the large hand folded on her stomach, even in sleep.

"Percy, there is also a change of clothes in the suitcase for you. I will call in the morning to find out how she is," said Denton as he handed Percy's cell phone charger to the old man.

"Try and sleep," instructed Maude and with that, the trio trudged once more to the old orange JPS truck.

"We only have enough gas to make one last trip up the hill, is there space to park the truck behind the house?" asked Joseph.

"Is over an acre of land, plenty of space, we might have to squeeze past the house but we can drive it right down to where we going to cook the pigs. If you not going home you will have to sleep in the truck," said Denton as Joseph maneuvered the truck once again through the hospital gates.

"Won't be the first time," Joseph replied.

"Come to think of it, I will also have to sleep in the truck, I have to give Miss Maude my bed tonight," said Denton.

"Bom bat!" screamed Joseph as they reached the Jacks Hill gate. "Bom bat."

Bom bat was Joseph's version of bumbo claat.

"Look at all those lights, the meter must be spinning like a gig and you know how much money Miss Carmen owes JPS? Do you have any idea how much money?" yelled Joseph.

"Just cool it man, by Monday morning all sea flat," said Denton smoothly as he climbed out of the truck.

"How you so sure?"

"Just trust me, just trust me."

CHAPTER 10

Preparations

The day of the party dawned sweet and clear. The dew was heavy on the grass and all was quiet at Jacks Hill Road.

Denton and Lipton had ended up sleeping in the back of the truck and Joseph was asleep in the cab snoring softly. Claude arrived early as planned to help dig the bar-b-q holes for the pigs. Having no idea of what had taken place the night before he was puzzled at the sight of the JPS truck parked in the back yard. He stood for a minute gazing at the truck then went to the tool shed for the tools. He decided that Denton must have had a hard night so he might as well get the holes done and the coals lit. He had brought some Pimento wood and allspice seasoning. They had picked a spot near to where the truck was parked and again Claude wondered what the hell such a big truck was doing parked in the yard. Claude could think of no reasonable answer and set about digging.

"You see how this man come here making dig, dig noise and disturbing my sleep," boomed Denton.

"AEEEEEIE!' screamed Claude.

Dropping the fork, Claude saw Joseph's head appear in the window of the truck.

"Boy you a idiat, you think a truck can talk?"

Denton and Lipton stood laughing, stiff from sleeping on the bed of the truck.

"Might as well get up now, in another ten minutes the sun would be up and too hot for us to sleep here anyway," said Denton.

Claude screamed at Denton, "If you frighten me like that again I leave here and don't come back!"

"Boy just tek the joke and let's find us some tea," said Lipton.

****

"Who is the whore at the dining table?" whispered Doris to Elizabeth, who was on her way to the bathroom.

"Lawd Jesus, day just light and she gone off already ...," grumbled Elizabeth.

"Is she one of Clifford's whores?" Doris asked, a little louder.

"No Grandma that is Auntie Margaret."

"Who? I don't know no Margaret, your mother found one of Clifford's whores. I am going for my stick," said Doris following Elizabeth to the bathroom door.

"Grandma go back to bed," Elizabeth told her grandmother and closed the door firmly behind her.

As Elizabeth sat, she remembered that today was the day of the party. She could not wait to get out of this house. She was tired of helping with the million and one functions her parents had, her grandmother was getting on her nerves and she could not get the new dress she had wanted for tonight.

She really wanted the dress. Her mother told her that even if they could afford it, the dress was too revealing for a girl her age. Elizabeth wanted to look older and sexier for Kevin. Unable to get his attention, she thought the dress would help. Although she had plenty of friends, she was bored with them. The boys her age just wanted to paw her and they had nothing interesting to talk about. Elizabeth dreamed of driving down Jacks Hill in Kevin's fancy SUV with the sun roof open. She would bake oatmeal cookies and they would go on picnics on the beach. Anyway, back to reality, she would have to wear her ratty old dress and look after the mad woman. 'Looking after Grandma,' she thought again, 'maybe I could have some fun with that'.

****

Maude was comfortable in the kitchen. She found her way around easily, knowing instinctively where Louise would put things. Maude loved the big kitchen with its center table and miles and miles of cupboard space. By the time the family started stirring she had made a large pot of cornmeal porridge and fried up a pile of Johnny cakes. There were plenty people to feed this morning and it was not a day to be fooling around with fried eggs and bacon or salt fish and ackee.

Louise had regaled Maude with stories of the family but today would be the first day that Maude would see them herself.

****

Carmen came downstairs prepared to do battle in the kitchen, she had no idea Louise had arranged for Maude to work. Margaret was close on her heels with the same thought. Instead they were greeted with the dining table set with steaming bowls of porridge, a large platter of Johnny cakes and a pot of coffee.

"What a strange breakfast," said Margaret biting into a delicious Johnny cake. "YUM!"

"Not really, ma'am," answered Maude, "The weather lady loves it, although maybe I should have fixed something else, it might call down rain."

Carmen sat grinning from ear to ear, her mouth filled with porridge, and looking at Maude as if she were an angel come down from heaven to rescue her.

"You are Maude," said Carmen.

"Pleased to meet you Miss Carmen," said Maude. "Louise ask me to help out today, so if you will excuse me, I have to feed Joseph, Denton, Claude and that apparition with yellow hair."

"Who is Joseph?" asked Margaret.

"Beats me, but if he is ok with Louise, he is ok with me," said Carmen, reaching for another fried dumpling.

"Well now that we have been relieved of kitchen duties, we can go to the hospital and maybe do some last minute shopping," continued Carmen. "We will have to fight the men for the car."

****

On returning to the kitchen, Maude not only found Denton, Joseph, Claude and Lipton but also the butcher, two pigs and the gentleman from next door who had brought over some tea bags. Maude was about to ask the gentleman to join the family for breakfast when he hurried through the kitchen door.

Puzzled, Maude wondered aloud what his problem was.

"Don't ask," said Denton, disappearing into the dining room to start clearing.

Marcia Moore telephoned Dunstan, it was early but she was frantic.

"Dunstan!"

"Yes Dear."

"What is it with you and this yes dear thing?"

"Marcia, you know that you wake me up again?"

"You sleep too much."

"I am an old man you know."

"Dunstan the dress for tonight can't fit me. It fit me last night and it can't fit me this morning."

"Marcia what did you eat last night?"

"Only 14 of the number 11 mangoes you brought me yesterday.'"

"So you want a dress?'

"Yes."

"I will pick you up at 10 o'clock."

"You taking bag of bones to the party?"

"It could never be my dear, sweet wife you talking about like that Marcia, you want the dress or not?"

"Yes I would like the dress, but who are you taking to the party?"

"You."

"Ok, see you at 10."

Shirley Metcalf had ten of her best dresses strewn around her bedroom. Alice was standing by with the iron awaiting the decision on Shirley's choice for tonight. It was such a long time since Shirley had been invited to a party and dress selection was a dilemma. Finally with Alice's help she decided on a tight fitted one shoulder number she had never had an occasion to wear. Suddenly, Shirley was no longer afraid to lose Kevin, and what's more, she was going to run his backside. She was tired of playing Rapunzel, and she planned on enjoying herself tonight. With mounting excitement, she picked up her car keys and headed out for her appointment at the hairdresser. She had booked for herself a full service day.

On her way down the hill she wondered why it had taken her so long to make her decision. Shirley felt as if she had been in a crazy half sleep since she had married Kevin. She had followed his instructions like a robot, mesmerized by his charm and good looks, so much that she had given in to his wish to not have children.

Maybe it had something to do with the goings on next door. Shirley could not help but hear the life that was playing out beside her door. Slamming car doors, shouting, laughter, even the dogs playing on the lawn revealed how drab and lonely her life was. 'Well,' she thought, 'I am going to fix that.'

****

The afternoon was warm and hazy, the heat from the fire was making Denton sleepy, he washed his face again. He was tired but he needed to keep going. With the loss of Louise and Percy, he felt the whole load was on his shoulders. He had to pull it off. This place in Jacks Hill was the first place in the world where he could rest easy. The family had taken him in somewhat reluctantly, but they had taken him in and for the first time in his life he felt safe and he felt loved. He wanted to see Louise but there was too much to do, he had spoken with Percy a couple of times and Percy had told him that Louise had been moved to a ward and that she was doing better today.

Denton was very relieved to hear the news and it gave him renewed energy. He needed to be sharp and have all his wits about him to do what was necessary later. Things were coming along nicely, he had just checked in with the kitchen, Maude had finished the potato salad and rice and peas was almost ready. The green salad was done and the dressing made. Claude and Denton were watching the chickens like mother hens. As soon as the chickens were in the oven to keep warm, Denton enlisted the help of Dan and Lester, who had been left at home to unearth the pigs and put them to rest. Every hour Denton said a prayer as he monitored the roasting, to see the crackling on the pigs and he knew his spirit would not rest until they were sitting on the party platters tonight. Then it would be time to feed and lock away the dogs and be showered and dressed in time to supervise the proceedings.

****

"You know when we have a party at home I have to do all this rass myself," announced Lester. "All is not what it seems sometimes," Dan replied, "but I must admit, it is very nice to have such faithful staff, I just wish I knew how I will pay them all for this."

"So what are your plans, what are you thinking of doing?"

"If talks go well tonight with the guy from ICW, the company will be absorbed into theirs, so technically I will no longer have a company but most of us will still have jobs. I still have to find about 10 million dollars."

"But why is that so if these guys are going to help you?"

"I have to get the house back Lester, and Carmen's car and a million other bills I have let slide. I don't want to move to Mona Heights although Carmen seems excited about it for some strange reason."

"I wish I could help," said Lester.

"You've helped enough, you have given us back Louise."

"Come on, Denton is calling us to see about the pigs."

****

Carmen and Margaret had been on the road for most of the day. They went shopping, although Carmen had little money for shopping, she enjoyed it nonetheless and they had gone to the hospital to see Louise. Unable to see Dr. Campbell, Carmen had to be content with what Percy had told her.

Louise looked a lot better today and having been moved to a ward meant she was out of immediate danger. Percy said more tests were needed to determine the extent of damage to her heart and the Doctor would let him know when the tests would be done. Until then, all they could do was wait. This did not sit well with Carmen and told Percy that if Dr. Campbell had not shown up by Sunday evening, she would flush him out for the details herself.

Louise acknowledged Carmen's presence with a nod and a smile but refused to speak. Percy, horrified that she might display her bad behavior to her employer, had tried to explain that Louise had shut down and that she did so all the time with him.

Carmen told Percy not to worry, in seventeen years she had seen many sides of Louise.

Back home, Carmen looked around and determined there was nothing to do. Denton had advised her to go to bed and stay out of his way.

Margaret listened to this exchange in shock. Everything was humming along smoothly and so she decided to shut her mouth and go to bed also. As soon as Margaret and Carmen had turned to go upstairs, Doris came rushing in from the study.

"Margaret, Margaret, my dear girl, when did you come?" asked Doris, her arms open for a hug.

"Mama you know it's me?"

"Of course I know it's you, come and hug your mother. Carmen, why didn't you tell me Margaret was coming?"

"Mama, I told you three times. Margaret came last night after you had gone to bed and this morning you shook your stick at her and called her Clifford's whore."

"No, no, no, no," said Doris, "don't listen to your sister, Margaret, she has an enormous bug up her ass and accuses me of the most terrible things. Between you and me Margaret, I think there is something wrong with Carmen."

Doris' Alzheimer's was slowly getting worse but she still had lucid moments. One just never knew when she would trip in or out. Doris was the reason Louise was still alive, she had recognized Louise's condition and told Percy what to do and now she clearly knew who Margaret was. A lucid spell could last anywhere from five minutes to half a day.

Carmen said to Margaret, "Let's not go to bed just yet. We should make use of every single minute that she is aware. Why don't we all talk in the study".

****

As soon as it was dark enough, Lipton turned the lights on. With so little to work with, he was pleased and surprised at how well it turned out. He was running late and needed to get dressed to help Denton. He had wanted to throw in the towel many times that day but loyalty to Denton had kept him going.

'We boys have to stick together,' he thought, as he gathered his tools. The boys from the strip had to help out each other; they were ridiculed and made fun of, sticking together was the only way to survive. For example, the lady of the house had returned this evening armed with a bottle of Just for Men and suggested he use it.

'Ungrateful bitch,' thought Lipton. 'I work my ass off from yesterday for free and all she can say is tone down my hair.' "They just don't get me ...," he muttered. "I wonder if the bitch know how much it cost me to bleach out my hair."

****

Joseph was in the kitchen with Maude. He had not returned the truck but had telephoned his boss, who was frantic with worry. He was so relieved to hear that Joseph was ok and that all the truck needed was gas that he mentioned nothing about firing Joseph.

"Just you wait, you think you escape? You big lug, as soon as your boss cool down and think again, he going fire you, mark my words," taunted Maude.

"You know Maude this is the reason why when I see you at Percy's I stay far from you. That mouth of yours is like a razor that can cut up man into ribbons."

"I did think you did not like me," she replied, sitting down and finally putting up her feet up on a chair. Everything was ready and they had a few minutes rest. Joseph also sat. He looked at Maude's feet and said, "They are so small. One would think a feisty woman like you would have bigger feet."

"Oh, so you are a foot man," said Maude, laughing.

"I don't know what you mean but I would rub them if they are hurting."

"Not now Joseph, we are at work remember, anyway they don't hurt, they feel tired. Lord knows they will be so tired after the party."

"So tell me something Maude. Would you pour hot oil down a man's earhole when he is sleeping?"

"No I would not Joseph, did some woman do that to you?"

"Yes, no, listen, Maude, would you like me to fix you something hot to drink?"

"I have a secret to tell you Joseph. Don't tell Louise or Percy," said Maude, getting up and standing as close as she could to Joseph.

"I like white rum and milk."

****

Upstairs Elizabeth tried to get her grandmother into a body shaper, one with extra boobs and plenty of bottom padding. Doris who had not been wearing panties rebelled, but after a promise of chocolate she consented. With the wig, makeup and body shaper, Doris looked younger. Elizabeth studied her handiwork and declared. "Mama, we going get you a man tonight."

"Don't be foolish girl, what would I be doing with a man?"

"Now Grandma you remember what you have to do when you need the bathroom?"

"Of course I remember," snapped Doris, not remembering one thing.

CHAPTER 11

The Party

Carmen observed herself in the mirror. She felt like a new woman. She looked like a new woman. Her black dress fit perfectly. Her hair shone, her curls bounced and her face glowed. She applied her lip gloss and reflected on her afternoon with Doris. She was almost sure it would be the last time Margaret and herself would spend with Doris in a lucid state.

After fifteen minutes, Doris's mind had begun to wonder, but in those fifteen minutes, the sisters told their mother how much they loved her. Doris had been alarmed at their gushing and had asked if she was about to die. They had assured her she was not and asked if she had any special wishes for her funeral when the time came. By then she had started to slip away but she had managed to say she wanted to be buried with her teeth in straight.

"I'm scared," said Dan suddenly and making Carmen jump.

She looked at her husband who was wrapped in a towel. "Hurry and get dressed, we need to be downstairs before the first guests arrive."

"Everything rides on this party tonight. I know Mr. Jenkins accepted the invitation to size up the family and see if we are good enough for his company. I would have to do a lot of entertaining if I got this position."

"Don't worry, everything will go fine, and if it doesn't, that will be fine too." Carmen twirled in front of the mirror.

Dan stared at her but said nothing.

"Dan, get dressed!" she scolded.

"You look beautiful Carmen, I have something to show you," he dropped his towel.

Carmen did not answer; instead she locked the bedroom door and took off her dress.

****

Claude was in his element, the bar was organized to the last glass and he had inspected the staff and ensured all shirts were clean and ties straight. He had pressed Joseph into service to fry the salt fish fritters and was extremely happy that Joseph did not drink and could be trusted to keep the batters separate. Maude hovered wanting to fry the fritters herself.

Denton could not stop admiring the pigs. Sheila would be served but Pat would grace the table as a centerpiece. Pat was golden brown with her crackling done to perfection. Denton thanked the god of pigs once more and stuffed a very red American apple in her mouth.

The only unhappy staff member was Lipton who kept mopping his brow and inspecting his hankie to check whether the Just for Men colour was running down his face.

Margaret and Lester came downstairs as the first guests arrived. There was no sign of Dan and Carmen so Bradley was dispatched to find his parents. The Patio was a sight to behold, the decorator from Stony Hill would be very proud of Lipton. The lights of Kingston mingled with the lights on the terrace. Stars hung low in the Heavens over the house high on Jacks Hill, making the night appear magical. It was as if nature had conspired with Lipton to put on a spectacular show.

There were no chairs, only cocktail tables, as the patio filled up, the guests were forced to talk and mingle. The atmosphere was amazing, completely conducive to relaxation and enjoyment. . Margaret and Lester moved through the crowd greeting guests and making excuses for Carmen and Dan. Bradley reported their bedroom door was shut tight. Denton and Lipton circulated with drink laden trays and Bradley's computer played appropriate music in the background.

****

One of the first guests was Basil Thomas. He was accompanied by Shelly Green, whom he had bribed with a promise to protect her job. Basil had on far too much cologne and as he sweated the smell grew stronger. Shelly fought for fresh air and tore herself away from him. Spotting Marcia and Dunstan by the bar, Shelly made a bee line for them.

"Are we the only ones from the office?" Shelly asked Marcia, trying not to notice Dunstan's hand resting on Marcia's bottom.

"Yes, I think we are," replied Marcia, between bites of fritters.

"Don't eat any more of those fritters or you will smell of salt fish," said Dunstan annoyed.

"Salt fish a top, salt fish a bottom," Marcia giggled. "You are going to eat some tonight so get used to the smell."

"Are you serious?" Dunstan gently squeezed her bottom, Marcia convulsed in more giggles.

"You hear that Wilfred?" said Dunstan to the thing in his pants. "If you let me down tonight, I chop off you rass and feed you to the dogs."

Grabbing a drink from a passing tray, Shelly turned to Marcia and pointed out Dan and Carmen who had just entered the room.

"Look at that woman," Shelly said to Marcia. "You see why you don't stand a chance?"

"Yes she is lovely, but have you seen the pig?" Marcia's eyes widened, "It's the best crackling I have seen in years!"

*****

Dan began to agree with Carmen's assurances for the last few days. A simpler life and Mona Heights was starting to appeal to him too. As he walked through the party he wished it would all soon be over. Not seeing Mr. Jenkins, he went to the front door to await his arrival.

Bradley had changed to dance music and people had begun to dance. The fritters were working their magic and guests no longer cared there were no chairs and that some of the drinks tasted funny.

When Basil Thomas saw Shirley Metcalf walk across the terrace, his heart stopped. He began to stalk her immediately but she was unimpressed at first. It took five fritters and a rum and coke before she had tumbled into his arms, where she felt so comfortable she snuggled in for the rest of the night.

"You have such a big voice," she whispered.

"Everything big, Miss," replied Basil as he pulled her tighter.

****

The party was in full swing and Margaret tried to coax 'Circle Food' away from the buffet table, but Circle would not budge, she stood clasping and unclasping the handle of her handbag. A few members of the Kiwi Club were at the party, 'Tight Bun' Betty was doing all she could to finish the Vodka and 'Scatter Teeth' was having a deaf eared argument with 'Thousand Teeth'.

Carmen kept trying to dodge them but they finally cornered her and demanded she say why she had stopped coming to club meetings, but before she could answer, they all became distracted by the arrival of Dan's special guest.

Gregory and Annette Jenkins apologized for being late. They were delayed at a cocktail party that ran on too long. Dan invited them in and introduced them to Carmen and Elizabeth, who had suddenly appeared with her grandmother. Dressed to the nines, the Jenkins looked out of place, as if they were to attend a ball and had happened upon a fry fish joint. Annette Jenkins was a lovely woman; she scrutinized the party and realized she would be able to relax with this crowd. Her husband Gregory was uncomfortable and stood as stiff as a light pole by her side.

Attempting to make polite conversation, he turned to Doris and said, "So are you Dan's or Carmen's mother?"

"I am mamma fowl," grinned Doris.

Unsure of what to make of her comment, Gregory turned to his wife and watched with horror as she stepped out of her high heel shoes and headed to the bar. A light tug on his coat tail made him turn once again in Doris' direction.

"Are you the man Elizabeth promise me?"

"I most certainly am not!" said Gregory sharply.

"Fucking hell," said Doris, "keep you drawers on, you are not that good looking anyway."

Denton was passing and overheard this exchange and diffused the situation with a drink order. He gently led Doris away and signaled Joseph to quickly order two fritters.

Telling Denton he needed a rather large Scotch, Gregory saw Annette coming back from the bar rather hurriedly all ten toes slapping the tile floor.

"Guess what?" Annette demanded.

"Annette I am in no guessing mood, I want to speak to Pottinger and get the hell out of here."

"Well, your son is the bartender, and he said not to tell anyone and gave me these for you," she said, as she pushed two fat fritters in his face.

Gregory had the uneasy feeling of one who had entered a mad house he automatically pushed a fritter in his mouth. Speaking with his mouth full, he felt like all sense of decency and decorum had gone through the window.

"Almighty God!! You could have let me have the first drink before you told me that!"

****

Elizabeth was watching Kevin, Kevin was watching Denton, and Denton was watching the time wondering if he should make his move now or after dinner. 'Now', he thought, 'everyone had a buzz on and if he waited until after dinner it might be too late'.

Now, if Kevin reacted badly no one would notice. Even Mr. Jenkins was looking as confused as a fart in a cane seat.

Denton handed the tray to Lipton and hurried to his room to fetch the documents. His stomach tightened with nerves and had a feeling to call the whole thing off, but he had gone too far to turn back now, plus he did not want to see the family he loved destroyed. Over his dead body would he allow Miss Doris and the dogs to be taken to Mona Heights.

Under the pretext of serving a drink, Denton pulled Kevin aside.

"Don't get upset, but here is the position, look at this paper," Denton handed a document to Kevin.

"You rascal, how did you get into my Zurich bank account?" Kevin demanded in amazement.

"I found the account number in your wallet and I figured out the pass word from all those things you love to cry out when we having a good time." Denton nervously shifted his tray from one hand to the other.

Slowed down considerably by the fritters and rum punch, Kevin rocked back on his heels and tried to look fierce.

"So this is the blackmail. You know, I have been expecting something since you took those pictures, but this is very devious Denton. You have transferred five thousand United States dollars of my money to the SOS children's fund, why?" Kevin exclaimed.

"This document is to prove to you that we have hacked the account and can move your funds around, while we were at it, we changed the password so you can no longer access the account."

"Get to the point and tell me what you want before I kill your rass."

"Don't kill me before you get your new password, any way it's not really blackmail, it's more like a sale."

"A sale!" Kevin's voice was rising as the enormity of the situation penetrated his intoxicated brain.

"I am going to sail your rass head into that wall shortly," he almost screamed, just stopping short as he saw Carmen coming toward them.

"Please circulate Denton," Carmen said, as she cruised by on her way to the kitchen. "I think it's time to serve the buffet."

"Listen quick Kevin, Mr. Dan has a boat at the Yacht Club and it's for sale. Give him a cheque for fifteen million dollars tonight. Tell him a story about why you want the boat, he won't care. He will be glad to get rid of it. When the cheque clears and he has his money, you will get back your account. Then and only then you can kill me but my Mama in Tivoli will get a picture of you with you tongue down mi throat hole. Capiche?" Denton felt very much like Al Pacino in 'The Godfather'.

"Rass …," said Kevin.

"Don't take it like that man we going to end up with a very nice boat. Think of the frolics we could have on a boat. I always hear Mr. Dan speak of moon light swimming at Lime Cay. Good times ahead man, just roll with it," and with that, he left Kevin to assist Carmen.

****

Pointing in Basil's direction, Lipton said to Claude, "Dancing deodorant says there is no Vodka in his drink."

"Oh God," swore Claude while keeping an eye on his father, "there is not enough Vodka, this is Jamaica or what?

"Why the hell them don't drink the rum punch?" Carefully serving a jigger of Vodka into Basil's glass, Claude wished he had another bottle. 'Tight Bun' Betty was coming for a refill soon.

She had been coming herself to the bar, her hands fluttering in his face as she wondered aloud to herself, what was such a nice boy doing tending bar. Each time he told her, "I love to tend bar, I am a bartender."

Claude had been trying to get his parents to understand that for years. He did not want to go to university, he did not want to be a lawyer, a doctor, an engineer, or heaven forbid join his father's insurance business. He wanted a bar. Give me the university money for a bar he had argued. "Over my dead body," was always his father's reply.

Claude's parents had also disregarded his sexuality. They acted as if it did not exist. They periodically searched his room for drugs and carefully monitored his moods. Never finding the slightest trace of drugs, they continued to pay for his car and gave him a weekly stipend.

Gregory and Annette had four other children, girls all younger than Claude and they had decided to concentrate on the girls and allow Claude to find his own way, after all, they could not hog tie him and make him study. Claude was sure of himself, he knew what he wanted in life and was so busy enjoying himself, he had no time for soul searching and temper tantrums. He was an even tempered, sweet child who came and went with no trouble. Handing Basil's glass to Lipton, Claude saw his father approaching the bar.

"Listen Claude," said Gregory, puzzled at the sound of his voice. He had a peculiar feeling that his voice was under water. "I have made up my mind, I am going to buy you the first bar I find in New Kingston for sale, but you must promise me to go there every night. I never want to buck you up at a party again."

It took Claude some time to get over the shock of what his father had said. He stood with the bottle of Scotch suspended in mid-air and stared at his father. "Dad, that's the best news ever. Don't worry, you will not regret it, there will be money," said Claude while refilling his father's glass.

"Well, tell me about these people, how do you know them?" asked Gregory.

"My friend Denton works for the Pottingers. Denton will do anything for them. He is accepted and loved in this house and Mr. and Mrs. Pottinger are good people Dad. When you treat people with respect and love, you usually get it back."

"And what exactly does Denton do for the Pottingers?"

"He is their gardener."

"You are bosom buddies with the gardener?"

"Yes dad."

"Oh my."

Suddenly feeling the need for fresh air, Gregory turned away from the bar.

He felt totally out of control and he did not like the feeling. Stepping high like a puss on hot-bricks, Gregory managed to negotiate the steps leading into the garden where he collapsed on the lawn in a heap.

'Where did I go wrong with that child,' he wondered, shaking his head, trying to clear it. He wondered if his mother was right. Old Mrs. Jenkins had repeatedly told him he was marrying beneath him. She had insisted things would turn out badly. As soon as the thought crossed his mind, he dismissed it. Annette had come from a highly educated family with little time for society. That was what rubbed old Mrs. Jenkins the wrong way. She had thought herself above them even as she knew she came from a direct line to the thieving Busha from Bluefields.

He gulped mouthfuls of the Jacks Hill night air. Gregory began to feel more like himself. 'Just in time,' he thought, as he righted himself and brushed off his pants. Dan Pottinger was strolling across the lawn towards him.

****

The food was delicious. Eat till you buss delicious. Marcia thought she had died and gone to heaven. Circle wished she had brought another handbag. Margaret was pleased. She was having a good time, as she dug into the potato salad for the third time. She knew she was going home with a least five extra pounds.

****

Carmen did not want to eat, she saw the others enjoying the food but she was full of her husband and had no appetite. Hunger would come later but for now, she was satisfied. Carmen circulated among her guests but no one paid her much attention, they were busy enjoying themselves, too stoned or too mellow.

Nearly all of the guests were friends of Margaret and Carmen, some friendships extended to their school days. She had had nothing to eat and hardly anything to drink, and was taken aback at the antics of some of her guests. Shirley Metcalf was holding tightly on to Basil as if her life depended on it and screaming across the fence to Alice for two bottles of Vodka. Carmen walked through the party picking up bits of conversation.

Lucy Thompson was saying to her husband Stuart, "I know you have been drinking. Do not lie to me!"

"You see any glass in my hand?" asked Stuart, holding his palms up for her inspection, While he braced himself against a large flower pot in which he had hidden a large glass of rum. Stuart Thompson had a compromised liver and was not allowed to drink. That did not stop him, he liked to drink, and his liver would have to cope. By the end of the party, Stuart would consume a bottle of rum, and Lucy would never catch him with a glass in his hand.

Standing next to Stuart was Judge Henry Logan. Judge Logan was having a deep and thought provoking argument with a Ficus tree. His wife Laura Ann looked on with a big smile, she was thirty years younger than him and as Carmen passed by she saw Laura Ann hand the Judge a fresh drink.

"And when I finished underlining the calls he made to her number in red pencil, the telephone bill looked like fucking Christmas paper," was the next snippet of conversation Carmen overheard. Patsy Blake was speaking of her husband, Dr. Tony Blake, who was ogling Elizabeth at the precise moment.

"When I confronted him," she continued to Glen and Marjorie Watkins, "He told me some rubbish about calls being work related. Can you imagine Marjorie, after Tony work all day with this nurse, he have to talk to her for twenty minutes at night?"

Carmen moved along quickly, she did not like that conversation, it brought back unpleasant memories and she was too in love with Dan now to revisit that episode. She saw Margaret and Lester with Ann and Vincent Chin and hurried to join them.

"Every day," said Lester in his loudest voice, "a chiney man get up, his first thought is, how am I going to fuck a niggar man today, eh Vincent, don't is true Vincent?"

The salt fish fritters were in total control of Vincent, who was in peals of laughter, water streaming from the slits of where his eyes should be.

Ann Chin was embarrassed and was fanning herself at about twenty miles an hour.

"Time for you gentlemen to eat," said Margaret. "Come along Ann; let us get them some plates."

"Vincent, come here my friend," boomed Lester. "Do not eat the pork, if you see what Rambo was doing with the pig you would not eat it."

"Shut up Lester," said Margaret.

"You shut up Margaret, just bring the chicken. Just chicken, you hear me Margaret, with plenty of sauce."

Watching Margaret and Ann walk towards the buffet table, Carmen saw from the corner of her eye, Dunstan trying to dance with Marcia. His arms could barely meet around her back. Dunstan was resting his head on her breasts and Marcia was sucking on a piece of crackling above his head.

CHAPTER 12

The Sale

Kevin Metcalf watched his wife reach across the fence for the Vodka. Completely sober, all traces of liquor and fritters had gone from his system in a rush of adrenaline. He decided it was time to rearrange his life. If he had to face the truth squarely in the face he could see that he had been unfair to Shirley. It is time now to let her go to make something of her life. He saw that he had been very selfish. He was tired of her now anyway, he would make it easy for her to leave but she would not be leaving with much.

As for Denton, he would think long and hard about how he would deal with him. Denton had forced Kevin into a difficult corner. This had come at a very bad time. Kevin had put a large amount of his client's money in that account along with money he was trying to launder. He absolutely had to get control of this account immediately; he waited until Shirley was back on the dance floor before going home for his cheque book.

Denton breathed a sigh of relief when he saw Kevin head in the direction of his house. He knew that Kevin was going for his cheque book. 'Tief from tief, God laugh,' thought Denton as he cleared dirty used glasses for recycling.

Denton's legs and back hurt and he desperately wanted to sit for a while and rest but he could not just yet. He was anxious to see Kevin give Mr. Dan the money. Denton knew he was playing a dangerous game, he could have walked away from the whole affair, it really was none of his business.

****

Elizabeth and Doris had also kept him extremely busy this evening. Finally, Elizabeth got the message that Kevin would never look in her direction, maybe it was the way Kevin kept running away from any contact with her. She noticed that he only wanted to talk to the waiters. Elizabeth did not suffer her heartbreak for long; as a matter of fact her heartbreak over Kevin lasted exactly five minutes. She became conscious of the way Dr. Blake looked at her and turned all her attention to him. He was not as cute as Kevin but he had a nice smile and a full head of shiny black hair. Giving a dance performance in which she gave the doctor flashes of leg and breast, she was ecstatic when she saw the effect she had on him. Denton later pulled her from the utility cupboard under the stairs where Dr. Blake was carrying out an examination of her breasts.

****

Unsupervised, Doris had full access to the buffet table and had been eating steadily for two hours when Denton finally caught her. Denton missed Louise sorely and wanted her desperately. He needed her help with this unruly family. Taking Doris to the powder room to clean her face, Denton sensed she would need the potty after grazing the table for so long.

He was far too busy to take her upstairs so he told her to use the toilet and left her in the powder room to do her business. In his anxiety to see Kevin conclude the transactions, Denton forgot all about Doris.

****

As Dan walked toward Gregory Jenkins, his anxiety returned. He saw Gregory stumble a bit and brush off his pants.

"Are you ok?" Dan asked.

"To tell you the truth, no," answered Gregory, "I feel a bit queasy for some reason. Let's sit on the lawn."

"No, I will get someone to bring us chairs and maybe you could use a cup of coffee?" asked Dan.

"Yes thank you that would be good."

Dan signaled to Margaret, who was closest and asked her to have the chairs and two cups of coffee sent down to them. Both men made small talk while they waited. Gregory complemented Dan on his home and Dan told him that it was no longer his home. An uneasy silence followed, they passed the remaining time admiring the view of Kingston below. When they were finally settled in, Gregory cleared his throat and said.

"Listen man, I see no reason to merge the companies, my offer is this. I will hire you, Thomas and the fat girl. We can work on packages later."

"But what about my clients?" asked Dan. "Don't you want me to bring my clients?"

"They will come, don't worry. I will give you two weeks to close and get rid of your baggage. You will report to Brian Wellington until I am sure I can make you a VP."

Dan hesitated so long that Gregory said. "I know you expected more but to be honest your company went down the crapper largely because of bad decisions on your part. I will give you five days to answer."

"Thank you Gregory, you will have my answer soon. I appreciate the offer," said Dan recovering quickly. He had not expected the abrupt manner in which the offer was delivered; he had thought there would have been a discussion and bargaining. Dan looked in the direction of Mona Heights and saw hundreds of twinkling lights and thought, 'Carmen will get her wish.'

****

The powder room in the Jacks Hill house was more than a powder room. Carmen once downstairs was reluctant to go back upstairs. She had outfitted the powder room with a full length mirror and cupboards where she stored her makeup and extra pairs of shoes so she could check and fix her appearance on her way out.

Doris looked around the powder room. The boy had left her in here to do something she could not remember what. She felt pressure in her bladder and looked at the basin and wondered what to do. She tried to climb on to the counter and after several attempts, she sat in the basin.

'This does not feel right,' she thought looking around. 'These things are so confusing.' Finally after several minutes, she saw the toilet and decided to try it. Carefully climbing down from the counter she faced the full length mirror and lifted her dress .Catching sight of her reflection, she stared at herself transfixed. Her pussy was gone. Someone had stolen her pussy. Clifford was going to leave her now for sure, he loved her pussy very much. It was the only part of her that he really liked.

Gone completely from her mind was the fact that Elizabeth had dressed her in a body suit and that her pussy lay beneath the smooth flesh coloured material. She started to cry, someone was going to pay, and she would get the police she had to find her pussy before Clifford asked for it.

*****

Carmen found Margaret at the bar.

"There is no dessert, we forgot the dessert. We were so busy concentrating on the food, we just forgot!"

"That's what you get when your gardener boy is your event planner," shot Margaret. "Mark you, this has been one swinging session, and I am enjoying myself so much I don't think dessert will be missed."

Claude having overheard their conversation, said to Carmen, "Miss Carmen, watch the bar for a minute, I will go to the car for my ice shaver. No one has been drinking the rum punch. We can do rum punch snow cones for dessert."

"There you go, Margaret, we have dessert. I wouldn't swap my event planners for all the gold in China!"

****

Dunstan was in constant dialog with Wilfred. Since Marcia had promised him the thing, or at least hinted at him getting it tonight, Wilfred had stood at attention and started to leak.

"Stop the blasted leaking Wilfred, go down and rest. I will need you to stand up later, don't tire yourself out!" said Dunstan to his Penis. But Wilfred paid him no mind and with every wiggle of Marcia's behind, Wilfred stood up stiffer than ever. Dunstan decided to take a break from dancing and talk to Dan. He had seen Jenkins leaving the lawn and although he could not see Dan's face, could tell by his walk he was not happy. He dispatched Marcia to get a snow cone and went to speak to his friend.

"Just cut and dry," said Dan to Dunstan. "No discussion about assets only that he was prepared to hire myself, Basil and Marcia, and that I had to get my shit together in two weeks."

"So what are you going to do?" asked Dunstan.

"I have no choice, I have to take the job, we will lose the house and the cars but I will be able to put food on the table and send the children to school."

"So you will need the Mona House?"

"Most definitely, I think we only have another ten days or so and then we will have to leave this one."

"This is one hell of a going away party," said Dunstan, "I can't tell you when last I have enjoyed myself so much."

A loud cheer went up from the crowd on the terrace as if in agreement with Dunstan's sentiment. The snow cones had revived them after dinner and the dance floor was rammed and the whole party it seemed was doing the electric slide.

"Oh God here comes Kevin," said Dan.

"Who is he?" Dunstan asked.

"My neighbor, nice enough guy but I have never been able to figure him out, he is kinda weird."

"Nice party Dan, can I speak to you privately for a minute?" he asked.

"Hello Kevin, thank you, I am glad you are having a good time, meet my friend Dunstan Watson, you can talk freely, he is a good scout."

Kevin shook Dunstan's hand and mumbled inaudibly. He turned to Dan and said, "I understand you have a boat for sale."

Dan's heart quickened, "Yes, as a matter of fact I do."

"Well," said Kevin, trying to maintain his cool, "I would like to offer you fifteen million Jamaican dollars for it. I have my cheque book here and it could be a done deal by morning."

For the second time that night, Dan was at a loss for words.

"It is worth much more than that, I am sure you know that," Dunstan piped in.

"Yes," said Dan, willing to accept anything for the boat. "If you can top that up a little, it's all yours."

"Seventeen." said Kevin.

"Twenty." Dunstan replied.

Kevin hesitated he wanted to tell them both to go to hell then go up to the house and stab Denton. In the corner of his eye he saw flashing lights and saw a squad car slow down at the gate.

"Done," said Kevin. "I will go into the light and write the cheque."

****

Denton stood at the edge of the terrace, his tray of glasses rattled. He watched the men on the lawn and tried to lip read. He saw the Commodore say twenty, but Kevin's back was to him and so had no idea what Kevin's reply had been.

He saw the squad car at the same time as the men on the lawn, and two glasses fell from his tray and smashed on the terrace. Too tired to bend down, Denton stood trembling. He was frozen to the spot, past the end of his rope.

Claude spied the cop car too and immediately looked for Denton. He saw him hunched over his tray and sprang into action. Abandoning the bar, Claude sprinted to Denton and relieved him of the tray and kicked the broken glasses into a bush.

"Denton, let's go," Claude said tugging at his sleeve. "We have to see what is going on at the gate." Hurrying down the driveway, they met the squad car at the same time as Dan and Dunstan.

"It's Sgt. Givans and Corporal Bailey," said Claude, relieved.

"Is the music too loud?" Dan inquired as he introduced himself and Dunstan.

"No, no we have come about some pork business," laughed Sgt, Givans.

"Ok," said Claude, "come this way, we still have half of one left."

"Are these boys in trouble?" asked Dan, concerned.

"Only if they don't have some dinner for us," replied Corporal Bailey.

"Ok, well enjoy," said Dan as he led Dunstan back to the party.

Kevin wrote the cheque with the light of one of Lipton's lamps. He felt cornered and cursed himself for being so stupid. At least he would have some value for his money, but that was little consolation, he was hopping mad. He looked at the unsigned cheque for twenty million dollars and wanted to tear it the hell up, but the feeling passed when he saw Denton laughing with two policemen on their way to the kitchen. He signed the cheque.

Passing Kevin on the driveway, Denton saw him writing and felt so relieved, it energized him. He could not believe he had done it. He must tell Louise. A large grin spread across his face as he escorted the officers to the kitchen.

****

Maude served large portions and sent Joseph for the drinks. Denton ate too, as he lifted the first forkful he realized it was his first meal that day. Sgt. Givans groaned with pleasure when Maude placed a large piece of crackling on his plate.

Denton felt revived after eating and thanked the officers again for their help and excused himself. He had to get back to work; he had guests to look after. Glancing around the kitchen on his way out, Denton thought of Miss Louise and was glad that he had ensured she would have her kitchen to come back to.

****

Joan Silvera held on to the cocktail table, she had been feeling strange all night. She had not minded and she was enjoying the feeling. She made a mental note to ask Carmen if something at the party had been spiked, then promptly forgot.

Joan had been on the dance floor all night. Her present boy-friend, Derrick Richards had gone to the bar for more drinks. Joan had been considering Derrick's proposal of marriage. She did not love him and he annoyed her immensely but she was shocked to find that after all these years she wanted to be Mrs. Somebody. She was tired of wandering around on New Year's Eve by herself, or going to parties and dancing with other single ladies.

The "I don't need a man, look at me I am woman," was a crock of shit. On a night like this Joan would allow Derrick to sleep over. She loved the way he helped her to undress and in the morning she looked forward to having someone to discuss the Sunday papers with. If she could only get him to stop lining up her shoes and ironing the bed linen while she was still in the bed, he would be perfect.

Joan let go of the cocktail table and steadied herself, she needed the powder room. Taking a few tentative steps she set off, weaving her way through the Cha Cha slide.

Joan wondered if she could get Carmen's decorator and bartender for the wedding. Shit the thought of a wedding sent chills up her spine. Rings and bridesmaids, cake and flowers …

****

Annette Jenkins had her ear pressed against the door of the powder room. "I hear crying," Annette told Joan.

"Do you know who is in there?" Joan asked.

"No," said Annette, "but I keep hearing the word pussy."

"Shut up!" said Joan.

"You listen," Annette stood back from the door.

"Oh God, it's Doris, I am going to open the door," said Joan.

They found Doris, her dress bunched around her waist, tears running down her cheeks.

"I've lost my pussy!" Doris wailed.

"Mama fowl," laughed Annette.

"Mama what?" Joan asked.

"She told us that was her name, I figured she had some sort of dementia," answered Annette.

"Come, Miss Doris, stop crying, I think I can help you find your pussy. Help me with her dress. Somebody has put this poor old lady in a body suit."

By the time they had sorted Doris and used the potty them-selves, Annette and Joan were like old friends. Doris, happy with the return of her lost body part, was now wailing that no one had fed her all day.

"I have decided to marry a man I do not love," confessed Joan.

"Love makes you do foolishness if he can dance and cook you can live happily ever after."

"So dancing and cooking is your recipe for a happy marriage?"

"Yes definitely."

"So where is your husband?"

"Oh he refused to dance so I sent him home."

CHAPTER 13

The Party ends

Louise opened her eyes and focused on Percy. He was propped up on his pillow snoring in the chair.

"Hi man, you should go home for a little."

"So you find your mouth again, I thought you had lost it," he yawned.

"Huh? What time is it?" she wondered out loud.

"Half past twelve."

"You know the party must be in full swing now. I am really sorry we missing it. Have you heard anything from Denton?" asked Louise.

"Yes, he called twice tonight, he said everything was going well but he was having a hard time with Doris and Elizabeth. He said to give you his love and kiss you and that he will come tomorrow to tell you every detail of the party."

"That's good I will look forward to that. I wonder if Joseph is in trouble."

"So you don't talk since you come in here and now past midnight you want to ask twenty questions?" Percy muttered in disbelief.

"I am feeling better Percy; you have a problem with that?"

"No my love," he said getting up to hug her and uncross her feet and arms.

"Joseph and the truck are still up the hill. Joseph spoke to his boss, who said he could return it on Monday. He needs gas for it and Claude promised to help."

"So what of Maude, is she managing?"

"Very well according to Denton but he wish you were there, he also said she and Joseph make a great team."

"A great team? Our Maude and Joseph?" Louise exclaimed. "You must be mad; those two don't like each other. Remember the wedding?"

"Yes I remember," he laughed. .

"This party kinda reminds me of the wedding, we did it with next to nothing, and if you forget Maude and Joseph, a fine time was had by all," she replied, as she closed her eyes remembering.

****

When Louise and Percy had left Maude, they moved to a single room on Brentford Road. Percy was determined to do two things, marry Louise and provide her with a house. Percy worked two jobs at that time. He was janitor for a firm on Marcus Garvey Drive and worked as a night watchman for an electrical company on Bell Road in the Industrial Estate, where he met Joseph.

Even working two jobs, money was never enough to get a house of their own, until the day Joseph had told them about a place on Herman Road where the owner was leasing land at a reasonable rate. Percy and Louise jumped at the opportunity and had signed the lease papers and slowly began to build.

When the house was completed to Percy's satisfaction he had proposed marriage on a Saturday morning while they were lounging in the Rockfort mineral bath. Louise said yes and promptly set about planning their wedding.

It was 1976, almost ten years to the day of their arrival in Kingston. The country was in an uproar and under a State of Emergency. The chaos was brought on by vandals who had set fire to a tenement building. Earnings from bauxite and tourism were at an all-time low and for the first time in Louise's memory, food was in short supply.

The first thing Louise had done upon getting home from the bath was to check her rice stash. She had only had about a pound in her pan and would need another ten pounds which meant at least five fist fights at the supermarket to get only two pounds each time.

A goat would be easy enough to get but she would need onions and garlic, two more hard items to get. A wedding cake would have to be made with Chiffon butter. Louise had sighed, even if they had to eat bulla cakes, she would marry her Percy.

Louise had knocked heads with Maude and together they stretched, carved, and cut the corners to make the meal work. The cake was delicious even with the wrong butter and little fruit. Unable to afford the traditional rum punch, Percy and Joseph had made a potent and delicious drink with Johncrow

Batty, honey and limes. This drink was called honey punch, as after two glasses, you found yourself searching for your honey.

Percy and Louise were married at a Little Church on Windward Road. The church sisters and choir had turned out in full force and the congregation had rocked with singing and clapping. The pastor called for heaps of blessings to be bestowed upon them and everyone agreed that the couple had been properly churched.

The reception was held at Herman Road and the whole yard was invited. A small contingency arrived from Bluefield's, driven in by Maude's brother Everton, a taxi driver. The entire yard had pitched in to help. They had all at some time felt the kind hand of Louise and they were happy to repay her in some measure.

Desmond Michaels who had lived closest to Louise and Percy had collected enough money and had engaged his cousin's Mento band from Port Antonio.

****

Maude sat beside Louise at the rickety head table made of blocks that supported an old door covered by a large white sheet. She had eased her tiny feet out of her uncomfortable shoes Louise had insisted she wear. She sighed and looked across the table at Joseph who was seated beside Percy.

The pastor had blessed the cake but had taken such a long time, her mind had wondered. She was aware she liked Joseph for a long time. He always seemed afraid of her and she knew it was her fault. Whenever he was around she had become abrasive to hide her true feelings. She did not know why except that she was afraid of his rejection and suspected that he did not like her.

Maude had lost track of time and the next thing she knew Louise was feeding Percy a piece of cake. Louise looked lovely. Her dress was made of white organza and cut on an a- line which made her appear smaller. There was no hiding her large hands, and as she shoveled cake into Percy's mouth, she had nearly choked him to death.

Desmond made a toast to the bride and groom and Maude had got lost in thought again. She remembered coming down the aisle behind Louise and Percy and her arm through Joseph's. She had caught his scent and her knees had buckled. Maude was afraid of the feeling. The last man who had made her feel that way had hurt her severely. She had no desire to go there again.

After the formalities, the Mento band started to play. The honey punch was working its magic. The sweetness of the honey and tartness of the lime hid the taste of the raw, unrefined estate rum. The church sisters who only hours before had been so pious were dancing in an ungodly fashion to a lively rendition of 'Where Did The Naughty Little Flea Go'.

Louise and Percy were happy, they had long felt married but it was good to have made it official. Maude watched the dancing for a while and reluctantly put her feet back in her shoes. Finally she had decided to hell with it and went in search of Joseph. She found him talking to a very pregnant Evadnie Williams who was happy to report she was carrying Joseph's baby. Maude became more caustic than ever.

****

Dan stood on the lawn staring at the cheque. God had answered his prayers. He was so thankful he stayed a while looking into the night sky and vowed to dedicate his life in service to his Lord and family. So focused was he that the noise of the party receded and he had not heard his wife talking to him until she hugged him.

"I am glad and I am sad," she told him, "This will mean no Mona Heights right?"

"You heard."

"Yes, Dunstan told me, poor man he could not contain himself, he is so happy for you."

"Well," said Dan, "this cheque has to be cleared before we allow ourselves to be too happy but yes this means no Mona Heights. We will be able to stop foreclosure on the house and allow us to get full value when we sell it. We will move, don't worry now we can take the time to do it properly and find an appropriate house."

"So what about Jenkins?" asked Carmen.

"Unfortunately the cheque is not big enough for me to tell him to go hump himself, so I will report to work. I want to save Basil and Marcia's jobs. That does not mean I will stay there forever. This money will buy us time, and pay our debts."

"Well before you get all maudlin and teary eyed, remember that Kevin also got a damn fine boat for a song," said Carmen, more sharply than intended.

Dan carefully folded the cheque and put it in his pocket. Carmen watched her husband, he was more relaxed and it warmed her heart how happy Dunstan had been for him. For her, it mattered little, she had found what was important to her and that money could not buy it. Linking her arm through his, she said, "Let's dance."

"I am into that!" said Dan, laughing for the first time in weeks.

Bradley decided it was time for people to go home. He needed his computer for more important things, he changed the music. He was conscious that the staff was wilting. Denton was on his last legs and Claude was cross eyed. Joseph on the other hand had taken on a second wind and was seen mixing a concoction with cow's milk and hurrying to the kitchen multiple times.

Bradley switched to his father's playlist and selected 'Good Night Irene'. He hoped the crowd would take the hint. No one moved. Bradley had to stop the music at 3:30 a.m. before people began looking for their hand bags and shoes.

"What a wonderful party declared 'Tight Bun' Betty and Carmen promptly confiscated her car keys.

Chatty Cathy who had not taken a breath or a drink in over three hours promised to pilot her home. 'Circle Food' snuck off earlier, her handbag stuffed to the brim. Patsy Blake who had said her good byes, waited patiently while Tony kissed Elizabeth good bye for the fourth time. The Watkins lingered at the steps talking to Margaret and Lester and Lucy Thompson was watching over Stuart, as he drank a cup of coffee. Dunstan tried to hurry Marcia along and Joan and Derrick sat nursing their last drink on the cold, wet lawn. Ann Chin tried to wake up Vincent who had gone to bed on the dance floor. The rest of the party were drifting away in the morning light, when they all heard loud laughter in the vicinity of Kevin and Shirley's gate.

Basil had reluctantly walked Shirley home. He did not want the night to end. He worried that history would repeat itself and after she had thought about him in the light of day, she would dodge him like the others before her. Cars were strewn on the road, they picked their way carefully to Shirley's gate which had been padlocked, even the pedestrian gate was locked.

"That's funny," said Shirley.

"Not really, you have been quite naughty," replied Basil.

"Áre you afraid Kevin might do something to you? Locking the gate means he is upset!"

"Nah," said Basil. "Look at me; men avoid even suggesting a fight with me."

"Miss Shirley, Miss Shirley," came a faint voice from a car on the street.

"That's my car!" said Shirley going closer. Alice was seated in the front seat of the car packed to the roof with clothes, handbags, and shoes.

"Come Miss Shirley, we can't get back into the house. He told me after I gave you the Vodka to start packing, but I was two steps ahead of him. I saw what was happening from your bedroom window, so I collected your rings and packed the trunk with your best silver and the good china before he asked me to pack," Alice breathlessly reported. "He took something from the safe and left it open so I got your jewelry box," she continued.

"I had some money," said Shirley.

"I am sitting on it," replied Alice.

"How did you find it?" Shirley wanted to know.

"Mam no ant moves in that house and I don't know about it. I know everything about you and all you business, so hurry and get in the car. Mr. Kevin is not a man to fuck wid."

And that's when Shirley started howling with laughter, not knowing why she was laughing, Basil joined her like a fool and they both made a racket in the early morning quiet.

"Did you bring the phone?" asked Shirley, wiping tears of laughter from her face.

"Yes Miss Shirley," Alice handed her the Blackberry.

"Put your number in this Basil, I am going to that new hotel in New Kingston; you know the one on the corner. Meet me for brunch tomorrow at twelve and we will figure out some things."

"Yes Miss Shirley," so happy he thought his heart would burst.

As they sped off down Jacks Hill Road, Alice wanted to know why the nice man called her Miss Shirley. "I don't know," Shirley replied, but he would call her that for the rest of their lives.

****

Carmen noticed Denton's limp; he was so tired he was walking sideways like a crab. Only hard core party people were left. It was almost five a.m. and the sky had begun to lighten. Carmen looked around; she would have to sweep the rest of them out. She stopped Denton in his tracks and made him put down the glasses he carried. She thanked him for everything he had done and assured him he would be rewarded in time.

Denton was asleep on his feet and did not hear a word. Carmen led him to the couch in Dan's study and made him lie down. She removed his shoes and covered him.

"Now I have seen everything!" said Margaret, who had been watching her sister. "I suppose the next thing you will do is breast feed him." Carmen laughed and together they checked on Doris and the children. Elizabeth was fast asleep on Doris's bed and Doris was curled in a ball beside her.

"I wonder what happened here," said Carmen. "Most of the time she hates her grandmother."

Bradley was another story. Fighting the sleep to the end, he was hunched over the computer downloading a game. Carmen had to physically close the computer and get him into bed.

Back downstairs, the sisters went in search of their husbands. Dan and Lester were helping Claude to pack his car. Annette Jenkins was seated in the front seat of Claude's car. Dan was telling Claude to check him next week for some money. Claude shook his head and said he had not done the party for money.

"It was very good of you to give Mrs. Jenkins a lift home. I thought I would have had to drive her myself."

"Don't worry Mr. Pottinger, we are going to the same place."

"Rass cleat, is she his mother!" Lester was incredulous.

****

Dunstan lay flat on his back wheezing like an old 1956 Buick. "Thank you Wilfred. Thank you man," Dunstan patted Wilfred on his small head. "I feel like I am going to dead but you did a fine job, I am proud of you."

Marcia lay snoring beside him, exposing her rolls of fat. Dunstan had a fleeting thought to his wife Del who was probably at home wondering where he was. The sun was streaming through the window of Marcia's small apartment. He was sure Del would be worried. Somehow he didn't give a shit and rolled over, closed his eyes and went to sleep.

****

Forty years of yearning passion was unleashed on Denton's bed that morning. Joseph and Maude split the headboard in two pieces and a leg had caved in and broken clean off the bed. Joseph had removed the mattress and placed it on the floor. He leaned the broken bed frame in a corner and wondered how

122

he would explain this to Denton. Maude was wide awake and watching his every move.

"You not tired?" Joseph asked her.

"Yes, but I am afraid to close my eyes, you might go away," she whispered.

"It's ok my love, I am not going anywhere."

****

Margaret, Lester, Dan and Carmen gathered in the kitchen for coffee. None of them were sleepy and they decided to fix breakfast. Dan kept repeating, "I can't believe it Carmen, I just can't believe it."

He removed the cheque from his pocket and inspected it for the hundredth time.

"By the time you get that cheque to the bank, it won't have any ink left on it," Lester laughed.

"It is such a relief to know I will be able to sort out the mess including paying Louise's medical bills," said Dan.

Margaret searched the refrigerator for left overs and said, "Boy those people were like vultures, not a damn thing left in here. Then, "bingo, some cornmeal porridge, enough for us all."

"Let's go to church," said Dan. "If we eat fast enough we can make the 8:15 service."

"You know that Lester is going to fall asleep and snore," said Margaret, already heating the porridge.

"God does not mind snoring," said Carmen as she got up to change.

CHAPTER 14

Two Years Later

Denton sat by Doris's freshly dug grave. He had picked the spot himself under the shade of a Guango tree but far enough from teifing Busha and his common law wife Matilda. Denton looked down the hillside and out to sea. 'Doris will love this spot,' he thought, 'a nice cool sea breeze all the time will make her rest easy'.

When Doris had died she was so small. Denton had carried her around like a baby. She died in his arms as he rocked her and sang, 'Nearer My God To Thee'.

Denton looked at the yawning hole and remembered after Miss Margaret's Party he had thought he was going to die, but he had had one last trick up his sleeve.

****

By the sea, Louise picked a bunch of sea grapes before going into the water. She trailed the grapes in the water and said her prayer before immersing herself. "Lord, I thank you for this ocean, I thank you for my life and I thank you for my Percy."

Tomorrow will be Doris's funeral but she would not be involved in the preparations. Miss Carmen had plenty help at the big house; Louise was enjoying her well earned rest and retirement.

Louise dug her toes into the fine white sand and watched dozens of tiny fish swimming around her ankles. She put the first sea grape into her mouth and sighed with contentment. Louise could not have imagined the turn of events in her life, she reflected on them often. While recovering from her heart attack, Louise had decided to return to Bluefield's to retire.

Dan stayed true to his word and had paid her medical bills including the angiogram that had put stents in her heart. He had offered to drive her to Bluefield's and Denton had asked to go along. He packed a bag with four swim suits and little else. Dan bought him a ticket to California but he kept putting off his date of departure.

Percy had gone ahead with a truck packed with their belongings. They planned to live in Old man Ossie's house with her half-brother until they could build a small house on their land. They also planned to sell some of their ten acres to build the house. With rent from Herman Road and their national insurance payments, they would be self-sufficient.

Having forgotten the exact location of the house due to changes that had occurred in her absence, Dan had driven slowly along the old coast road, when Denton saw a sign that read Morgan's Estate House for sale. Squealing with excitement, Denton had asked if that was Busha's place. Louise did not know but Percy would be able to tell them.

Percy confirmed that Busha's house and what was left of the land were for sale.

Denton and Percy had told Dan and Carmen about Busha and at the end of the story; Dan had become so intrigued he had driven up the hill to have a look.

Busha had left behind a rightful wife and two children, George and Rachel in Scotland. Having grown without their father, the children were suspicious and resentful of the man who had abandoned them with a sickly, nagging, and irritating mother. Busha had willed most of his estate to them but George vowed never to visit the country that had robbed him of a father. He had tried to manage the estate from Scotland later conceding it was a huge mistake. The estate deteriorated in no time. Matilda had four sons during the years she had lived with Busha but none of her sons had inherited a Scottish freckle, pale skin, or a Scottish blue eye. They all bore a strong resemblance to the Methodist Minister and Busha had not left them one cent. Each of the boys had been hired by George to run the Estate and each one did more damage than the last.

The house was falling apart, all farm animals had been stolen and weeds and woodland had slowly encroached on the house. Dan had fallen in love immediately. Carmen saw the look in his eye and wailed that the house was too big.

Denton walked the property and thought, 'Dear Lord what have I done? I was only curious. There is not one decent night club for miles.' Louise had also seen the look on Dan's face and smiling to herself, she thought it would be nice to have her family nearby.

The pending funeral brought back a flood of memories. Louise floated in the water and remembered how she had cried when Denton told her about what he had done to Kevin. She cried until Percy started to worry. Louise was sure Kevin would have her son killed; anyone listening would have thought she had given birth to Denton herself. Percy went on one of his rants and told Denton that under no circumstance should he get onto that boat with Kevin or risk ending up as a shark's dinner. Denton was moved by their obvious distress. He hurried to reassure them that he had one last ace up his sleeve. To this day Louise still wondered what it was.

The funeral was held at the Anglican Church in Savanna-La-Mar. Denton cut a fine figure in his new suit as he sat in the family pew beside Elizabeth and Bradley. Denton was the only one who cried for Doris. Her daughters were dry eyed and relieved that the ordeal was over. Fighting back tears, he had looked across at Elizabeth and Bradley. He was proud of them. He had held the incident in the utility cupboard with Elizabeth and Dr. Tony as a stick over her head. Threatening to tell, he had forced her to study until she had gotten straight A's. Elizabeth was now at college in Florida and living with Margaret. Bradley was at Monroe school for boys. Denton discovered that after their computer fraud, Bradley had taken things to a higher level and had become a fully-fledged computer thief, downloading and accessing everything from porn to school books. He was spending so much time online that it had been easy for Denton to convince Dan and Carmen that the solution for getting the boy to sleep would be to send him to boarding school.

Denton was happy to see Bradley looking rested, relaxed and without that lost and glazed look in his eyes. As the organ played the last hymn, Denton felt tears fill his eyes. He remembered the day on the back lawn with the dog shit hose and felt the tears run freely down his cheeks.

Carmen and Dan, Margaret and Lester could not believe so many people had made the long journey to attend the funeral. Some Kiwi members hired a bus, but that was understandable those ladies loved a good funeral. As long as a member was remotely connected they hired a bus. Sometimes these ladies did not know the dead or their family. If the deceased was an important person, you could count on seeing them, safe in the knowledge that the dead would not inquire.

Basil and Shirley Thomas also made the journey despite Miss Shirley being seven and a half months pregnant. Dunstan and Marcia also came. Dan was alarmed on seeing Dunstan. Dunstan looked gaunt and drawn, with dark circles under his eyes and noticeable weight loss. When Dan had enquired Dunstan shrugged off his question and said he was fine. In truth, Dunstan was not fine. Marcia and Wilfred were slowly killing him. Joan Silvera sent her condolences; she could not attend as she was suffering from third degree burns to her bottom.

Having seen Miss Doris to her final resting place, the mourners gathered at the old estate house. Dan and a somewhat reluctant Carmen (she still had romantic fantasies of the double bed in Mona), had slowly started converting the house into a small hotel. They had six rooms available and with little advertising the rooms were booked solid. Dan was in debt again but there was light at the end of this tunnel and he was the happiest he had ever been.

Denton cashed in his ticket to California and became the bell captain, head waiter, grounds supervisor and chief consultant.

There were many signs of construction but the guests enjoyed the beautiful grounds and fine old house. Hotel guests mingled with mourners, the atmosphere was subdued and quiet. People talked in hushed tones as if Doris was in the next room.

The sun set over the sea and bathed the garden in a soft orange light.

The Kiwi ladies were taking inventory of the house and grounds. There had been lots of talk at the club about the

Pottingers falling on hard times. They had been curious to see for themselves just how Carmen and Dan had fared. 'Scatter Teeth', an authority on all things was telling the group that the house had been built in the bungalow style.

A style invented by the British to build houses in India to keep out the heat. Notice, she continued that the walls were thick and the house surrounded by a large verandah, note the high roof that overhangs on all sides, another trick to manage heat. If you follow me inside we will be sure to find an attic and storerooms in the roof, also made to trap the heat.

Call me Pearlie said "Call me Pearlie!" when she realized the dining room was at least five degrees cooler than outside. They were standing in front of a large portrait of Busha that Dan had sent to Kingston to have restored when Carmen caught up with them. When questioned about the portrait, she evaded the questions as best she could, but she did tell them that they had had a million arguments about hanging the portrait in the dining room. She was certain the old and ugly white man was giving them all indigestion. The ladies were awed by the rich mahogany panels and gleaming Purple Heart flooring, the cool crisp white linens and spots of colour provided by the art work. Carmen was proud and found herself at last falling in love with the old house.

In the kitchen there was talk of duppies. Maude who was in charge in the kitchen was telling Denton she would lend him a pair of her red panties to stop Miss Doris' ghost from interfering with his willy. Denton was arranging a tray of sandwiches and retorted that Miss Doris' duppy was not the one to be concerned about. She should keep her red panty for the nights Joseph went to Montego Bay to meet the guests. Louise sat idly by munching on peanuts, she added that they needed black panties and not red. Percy tried to get to the peanuts and dust off the salt before Louise could put them in her mouth.

Life was good.

The Daily Gleaner, Saturday July 7, 2012

MISSING BOAT FOUND BY TEENAGERS SCUBA DIVING

Teenagers diving near Bushy Cay found the missing Bertram belonging to Kevin Metcalf, a prominent lawyer who has been missing for two years.

The search for Mr. Metcalf and his boat man Vaughn Miller was called off when it was discovered that sums of money belonging to Mr. Metcalf's clients had gone missing.

After a thorough examination of the boat, Navy Engineering Officer Lewis reported that the fuel lines had been cut.

ABOUT THE AUTHOR

Jacks Hill Road is Jennifer Grahame's first novel. She is a painter, currently studying Visual Arts with Professor Eugenio D'Melon.

Jennifer lives in Kingston, Jamaica.

Reach out to Jennifer:

Website: http://www.jennifergrahame.com/

Coming Soon!-Summer 2013

Sex and Scrambled Eggs

Nadine is approaching her 40th Birthday. With one disastrous affair behind her, she decides to look for another man before her clock stops. After some months, Nadine comes to the conclusion that she must either rob the cradle or the grave.

Join Nadine on her frantic search through the length and breadth of Jamaica for a suitable man.

Made in the USA
San Bernardino, CA
10 August 2016